CERTAIN DARK THINGS

CERTAIN DARK THINGS

STORIES

M.J. PACK

Thought Catalog Books

Brooklyn, NY

THOUGHT CATALOG BOOKS

Copyright © 2015 by The Thought & Expression Co.

All rights reserved. Published by Thought Catalog Books, a division of The Thought & Expression Co., Williamsburg, Brooklyn. For general information and submissions: manuscripts@thoughtcatalog.com.

First edition, 2015
ISBN 978-0692551349
10 9 8 7 6 5 4 3 2 1

Founded in 2010, Thought Catalog is a website and imprint dedicated to your ideas and stories. We publish fiction and non-fiction from emerging and established writers across all genres.

Cover photography by © iStock.com/TexPhoto
Cover design by Nick Kinling

IN MEMORY OF MY DAD

I hope I've made you proud

Contents

To my mother, who never stopped believing in me or discouraged me from playing on the dark side.

To my husband, for supporting this crazy dream of mine and sparking to life a passion I'd thought long gone.

To Chrissy and the rest of the Thought Catalog team, for giving me the opportunity to do what I've always wanted to.

And to you, dear reader, without whom none of this would be possible.

ALIVE

———————

Some people spend their whole lives bored. They might not even know it, but they are. They get up in the morning, go to work, head home, eat dinner, go to bed – this same tired routine playing out endlessly, endlessly, day after day until they find themselves in the ground. Some people will never realize they wasted their life until it's already over.

Not me. I lived my life to the fullest. I did everything I ever wanted to – ate the finest foods, traveled to exotic lands, slept with beautiful women – because I understood what most people don't. I knew that everyone is handed this one chance to experience the world as it spins in the darkness of space, but more importantly I knew that you only get so many spins.

I have my first wife to thank for this. It will surprise some of you to read those words but this is my last chance to share my story; I am an old man, the cancer has taken control of my insides and some stories can only be told when the teller isn't around to face the consequences.

None of you, no matter how well you think you know me, know the truth about what happened to my first wife Miranda. I have held this from you like the dirty thing it is, something dead and rotting that should've been buried long ago, but the fact remains that I didn't tell you because I felt it was my burden to bear. There is something so deliciously terrible about being the sole keeper of a secret – the tug-of-war between sharing what weighs on your soul and keeping it as your own dark companion forever.

———————

I married Miranda in the spring of 1946. We were as young and bright as new blossoms on the trees. I loved her so desperately because she was what I could never be: outgoing, vivacious, captivating... to put it short, she was a star. Even at 18 Miranda could walk into a room and all eyes would turn to her. It wasn't so much that she was beautiful – of course she was beautiful – but there was something about her that seemed to radiate from within, like she had a fire burning in her belly. She was special. She was meant for more than our shitty little railroad town and yet part of her charm was that she didn't seem to know it. Miranda was like Jean Harlow had dropped from the sky, landed in a cornfield, and then went about her business as though nothing extraordinary had happened at all.

Sometimes when we were lying in bed I would just stare at her. Sleeping, serene, and yet all the while smoldering with that flame that resided inside her like magic. I brushed the hair from her face. I wanted to give her everything even though I had nothing to give, nothing that Miranda truly deserved.

Instead I built a small but modest life. We had a nice, clean house near Main Street so she could shop for dresses whenever she wanted. I held a respectable job selling insurance policies at my father's office. I took her to nice dinners at the local diner and movies down at the drive-in.

It took me a while to notice, but the flame in Miranda began to burn her from the inside out. I could see it in her face when she was the most glamorous woman at any of our company cocktail parties; she could outshine the rest of them without even trying. She no longer relished all eyes turning on her when she entered a room because it was only expected, as natural as breathing. Of course my coworkers wanted to fuck her. Of course their wives hated her. Of course there would be petty gossip and dirty talk but none of it mattered because it was so goddamn easy.

We had only been married for five years when I walked into our bedroom and there she was, sitting at the edge of our bed with a half-empty martini in her hand. I had left work early, hoping to surprise her as she'd seemed down in the dumps as of late, only to find that she'd been drinking since I left that morning.

"God, Arthur," she said, her voice lubricated by cheap gin, "I'm so bored. I'm so godawfully bored."

The martini glass tipped dangerously in her hand. I made a slow move towards her, afraid she might bolt like a stray cat.

"Darling, let me have that."

Miranda jerked away even though I'd made no attempt to touch her. Gin sloshed over the edge and soaked into the carpet near her bare feet. Her toes were painted red, I remember – don't we remember the strangest things?

"I h-hate this place." Hiccups were setting in and this was a fresh shock; my wife was always cool, collected, never so much as a burp or a giggle at the dozens of cocktail parties I'd taken her to over the years. (Dozens, I realized then? Had it really been dozens of those office get-togethers I'd dragged her to? I thought at that moment yes, she was right, those *had* been terribly boring.)

"I hate it here, I d-d-don't belong here, Arthur." Miranda noticed the martini glass was spilling and she righted it only to take another deep sip. Swig, was the better word. "I'm like – a – a rose you planted in one of those states where it never gets warm. You want me to be beautiful here but I can't. I'm wilting."

And then she began to cry, which scared me more than anything. I hadn't seen my wife cry since our wedding day and even then it had been only a single tear running down her cheek, probably because that was the most glamorous way to cry, and with Miranda there was always someone watching her, there was always a spotlight as though her life was a silver screen and the rest of us just blurry figures in the audience.

If this had been a scene in the movie of her life any discerning director would have left it on the cutting room floor. It was not elegant, the crying was not pretty, and she was spilling more gin on the carpet.

The next day I booked a trip to Manhattan. I couldn't promise her that we could leave Nebraska, not yet, we didn't have the money but I had enough squirreled away for a jaunt to somewhere a winter rose could thrive.

Miranda was ecstatic. She bought four new dresses, a new luggage set, shoes and jewelry and expensive makeup. I let her do it because I wanted her to be happy and in all honesty I thought she'd get it out of her system.

I'll never forget the way she looked when we saw Times Square for the first time. The way the streetlights sparkled in her eyes. Her pretty face turned up to take it in, to take all of it in, the sights and sounds and smells and good god, I don't think I've ever seen her more beautiful.

That first night we made love the way we hadn't in a very long time. I supposed I hadn't even realized it, how she'd been pulling away from me for much longer than my stupid self cared to pay attention to. Because maybe it wasn't just Nebraska that was boring, you know?

It was only our second afternoon in Manhattan. I had planned to take her to a nice four-star restaurant on the main drag, something really nice for lunch, my belly was already growling just thinking about how much better the food would be from our local diner's. The flow of people was thick that day, everyone was out and about and it was exciting the way our hometown never could hope to be. That sense of being part of something simply by standing in a crowd. It's something I've experienced many times over since then, but that day was the first.

She was holding my hand. Her fingers were so thin, so delicate inside her elegant glove. I loved how they felt in my palm. I always had.

I gave them an affectionate squeeze as I watched for the traffic to slow so we could cross the street. Then, all at once, everyone started to move. I felt myself trapped in the rush of bodies like a leaf caught in the wind; I tightened my grip and turned to look at Miranda just as I realized my fingers had closed around nothing but cloth.

I glanced down at my own hand to see it holding her glove. I looked up, hoping to find her only a few people behind, but there were so many faces and none of them were hers.

I called her name once, twice as the crowd crushed me towards the other side of the street. It was a blessing because if they hadn't I'd have stayed in the center of the road, screaming for Miranda as the impatient New York traffic grew tired of my antics and eventually ran me down.

Lunch forgotten, I crossed to where we'd started as soon as the cars allowed. Some part of me had this wild idea that maybe she'd just spotted something in a store window she simply had to have, some sparkling trinket that she wanted and I'd find her there, hands pressed against the glass – one gloved, one not – and when I approached she'd look up, give me that beautiful movie star smile and ask pretty please, Arthur, will you get it for me?

I backtracked all the way to our hotel. She wasn't at any of the shops.

In our hotel room (where she also wasn't) I went straight for the phone to call the police. She'd been taken from me, Miranda was missing and I needed help, but it was as I reached for the phone that I realized something.

The jewelry box, the one she had filled with new earrings and necklaces and other baubles just before we'd left – far too many for a few nights in Manhattan, I'd thought vaguely at the time – was gone. A quick peek into the drawer near my side of the bed proved that so was the envelope of emergency cash I'd hidden inside the Gideon Bible.

I sat on the edge of the bed. Had a martini been in my hands, I would've spilled gin on the floor.

I'm not sure when I actually called the police. I think in a blind moment of rage I'd meant to report her as a thief but when they arrived, neat and stern in their blue uniforms, I found myself telling them that my wife had been taken from me in a crowd. I showed them the glove she'd left behind. I described her in the most clinical of terms; I told them the color of her hair (blonde) and her eyes (blue) and I never mentioned the way she burned from the inside.

Maybe it was easier that way. To tell them she'd been taken. Maybe I was embarrassed. Maybe some part of me still believed it, despite the missing valuables. Maybe in my heart I couldn't face the fact that the beautiful, bored woman I loved had left me like a fool in the streets of Manhattan, had perhaps been planning to leave from the first moment I showed her our plane tickets to New York.

On my flight back to Nebraska, short $300 and one wife, I could hear her voice in my ears. I'm so bored, she'd said. I'm so godawfully bored.

I made myself a promise then. I wasn't going to let her destroy me. I wasn't going to let her be right. I wasn't going to be boring anymore.

Rumors run rampant in a small town when there's nothing else to talk about but each other. I didn't hear the stories they told about me, but I can only imagine what they came up with. For all I know they thought Miranda had left me for Clark Gable and was already ripe with his bastard child. The explanation had to have been as grandiose as that for me to tender my resignation to my furious father, sell my clean little house with everything in it, and head out on the road with only the cash in my pocket and Miranda's abandoned luggage set filled with what little possessions I had left.

Before going, though, I took all her dresses to the backyard. I soaked them in gasoline. I lit a match.

Silk and satin and lace... it all burns so quickly.

Some of you reading this must be saying, yes, we know this part, Arthur. Eventually you were honest with us and you were honest with yourself and you told us Miranda ran away in Manhattan. This is no secret.

This is not the secret.

I spent the next 10 years of my life doing what some people only dream of. Anywhere that sounded interesting, I went. Any woman that caught my eye, I wooed. Nothing was out of the question. I worked odd jobs (some odder than most) to make a living as I traveled the world. Having worked in insurance I knew how to minimize risk and yet took every one that crossed my path.

You know, after all. You've seen the pictures and souvenirs.

One cool spring day in 1961 I found myself in New York again. It wasn't something I'd planned – I'd hopped a train and somehow, there I was. Before I knew it I was standing at the same intersection of Manhattan where my wife had slipped her hand out of mine, leaving me with only a glove and my own suffocating boredom.

Looking at the people as they crossed the street, I expected to feel angry. God knows I'd been angry when I left Manhattan the last time. I searched my soul for that anger, that rage I'd struggled with for the first few years of my new life, and found only a strange sense of peace.

"Thank you, Miranda," I said. I was smiling. A pretty girl passed me, saw my smile, and returned it. She was nowhere near as beautiful as Miranda had been but something I'd learned was that women who burned from the inside were hot to the touch. Those women, they scalded you. Sometimes a flame in your belly is just an excuse for arson.

I had no desire to explore Manhattan – in all my travels this was one place I had (perhaps unconsciously) avoided – but there were no trains out of town for another day so I wandered aimlessly out of the city. I liked to let my feet lead me where they may; I have found some of the more interesting places that way.

That day my feet led me to Coney Island. It felt right immediately; something about the bright colors and circus atmosphere was somehow a soothing alternative to the glaring lights of Manhattan. I ambled down the boardwalk for a bit, sipping a beer. I rode the ferris wheel. I ate a hot dog.

I had just decided to head back to the train station when I spotted it: a big blanched structure that resembled the front of a carnival funhouse. A booth sat in the center, surrounded by signs that screamed various promises at passersby.

IT'S ALIVE!
A MYSTERY OF NATURE!
KEPT ALIVE THRU THE MIRACLE OF SCIENCE!
YOU WON'T BELIEVE YOUR EYES!
IT'S ALIVE!

The repeated claims that whatever dwelled inside the white trailer was ALIVE reminded me of Barnum & Bailey's fiasco, similarly screamed promises painted on signs that lead paying customers into a dark room only to find a mummified monkey torso fused to a tuna's tail. It had been advertised as a mermaid and while it was clearly not, people seemed angrier that the subject was dead rather than a scam – as though a live woman with a skirt for a tail would have been a better deal.

I approached the trailer and the booth at its center where an uninterested old man waited inside, flipping the pages of a comic book with callused thumbs. Another sign on the front of his booth read AS REAL AS YOU OR ME!

"Excuse me, sir," I said, "what is this?"

He jerked one of those thumbs upwards, not looking at me.

I leaned back to see a big sign above his booth and couldn't be sure how I'd missed it. In huge, proud letters, it read:

LADY ALLIGATOR!

It's ALIVE, I thought inexplicably.

"One, please," I said, putting my money on the counter. Without breaking eye contact with his comic he took the coins and slid a ticket towards me. He licked his callus and turned another page.

I began to go inside, then paused. The day had grown almost eerily quiet. The boardwalk had emptied out and I couldn't see anyone else frequenting any of the other smaller freak show trailers.

"Slow day?" I asked, and he shrugged.

Not wanting to bother him further I walked up the stairs to the right of his booth. They led to a corridor that turned a corner, leaving behind the dull sunlight of the spring day and plunging me into darkness.

A sudden acrid smell struck me. It was not unlike the vague scent of shit that seems to surround the three rings of a circus, but something else was there too, an oddly alluring undertone of perfumed oils. The two odors struggled for dominance and neither could get the upper hand, leaving the trailer smelling of an uncomfortable animal sexuality.

I groped along the wall, determined not to let the cheap scare factor get to me. It was how they did things, these carnies, they robbed you of your basic sense of safety so they could take you off guard when their sham freaks finally made an appearance. I wondered if they'd painted Lady Alligator green for the right effect and laughed breathlessly.

As I shuffled along I saw a flickering orange light around an upcoming corner. *Nearly there, then,* I thought, and the smell suddenly hit me in a staggering gust. Carnal, somehow disgusting and yet I felt an unexpected stirring in my pants. My mouth had gone dry.

When I turned the corner I was surprised to see the room filled with burning candles. At their center, lit ominously by their shuddering glow, was a large porcelain bathtub.

I had stopped when I entered, surprised first by the number of candles, but I found myself unable to move when one long, slender leg emerged from the tub, pointing prettily towards the ceiling.

The skin on this leg was mottled, scaly. Only the sole of the foot was smooth, giving it a strangely virginal look. It wasn't green, though that was a small comfort.

The leg disappeared back into the tub and two arms slid slowly out, resting on either side. The skin of the arms were just as spoilt as the skin had been on the leg; the fingers began to drum along the porcelain and I saw their nails were long, sharp. An unsettling tap-tap-tapping noise filled the room.

I realized I'd been holding my breath and took in a great, gasping gulp of air. That was a mistake; I nearly gagged on the smell.

The thing in the tub made a low, rumbling sound in the back of its throat. I felt for an insane moment that it was calling to me.

My feet felt like they were filled with lead but I took one step forward, then another. I forced myself to move until I was standing at the center of the room, facing the bathtub and the thing inside.

It turned its head towards me.

I tried to scream. I tried to scream and nothing came out because it had fixed me with its gaze and I was frozen like a mouse cornered by a rattlesnake.

The skin on its face was as mottled and destroyed as I'd seen on its limbs; webs of damaged tissue ran along the cheeks, forehead, jaw like hot wax had been poured there. Where the nose should've been were two sunken slits like the holes in a skull on display in a science classroom. Its long hair was plaited in a strangely elegant braid that rested on one shoulder; I couldn't tell the color, the candles gave the whole room an alien orange glow, turning everything into a smoldering sort of amber. The tops of its breasts swelled above the murky water in twisted mimicry of a pin-up girl posing in a bubble bath. I was struck by its contradiction, a thing of both revulsion and raw sensuality.

Then it smiled at me.

When it did, its lips split into an impossibly wide grin; it was so terrifying, so awful to behold that it took me a moment to realize the flesh there had, at one point, been slit beyond the normal reach of a human smile. The corners of its mouth had the shiny-smooth texture of healed-over skin and now the grin could extend almost to its misshapen ears.

Its teeth had been filed to sharp points.

I was seconds away from turning to leave the monster in its grotesque glow of candlelight when it said,

"Hello, Arthur."

I knew that voice.

I *knew* that voice.

Oh, dear god, I knew that voice.

I tried to say her name but all that came out was a low *mmmm* noise.

Lady Alligator drummed its sharp nails along the porcelain edge of the tub again. I felt the sound in the depths of my soul.

"I suppose I knew you'd find me someday," it sighed, stretching luxuriously. "After all, I'm sure it's all you've been doing. Looking for me."

I thought of when I'd burned her clothes in the backyard and said nothing.

Lady Alligator cocked its head, surveying me with the same bored impatience I remembered so well from my few young years as a husband. Its eyes above that slitted, inhuman nose... they were Miranda's, there was no mistaking that, and I think perhaps it was the worst part, that though the rest of her had become a monster the eyes hadn't changed at all.

"Say something, Arthur." Not a suggestion. A demand.

"What – what happened to you?" I finally managed. It sounded monumentally stupid even as it left my lips but I could think of nothing else. "Who did this? Who did this to you?"

Lady Alligator rolled Miranda's eyes.

"Oh, Arthur," it said, disappointed in me as always. "You're so naïve."

I took my suit jacket off and held it towards her. To cover her up, you see, because it didn't matter that 10 years had passed, it didn't matter all the time I spent convinced she'd left me in the streets of Manhattan, it didn't matter that I thought I had changed because I hadn't, I still loved her and I thought I could save her.

"Stand up, Miranda, put this on, I'm getting you out of here."

Lady Alligator stared at me. It didn't move.

"Come on, Miranda, we're leaving."

"What, like this is one of your dreadfully boring cocktail parties and you've had your fill?" it said with a barking little laugh. "I'm still the pretty wife on your arm and you can shoo me out the door because you've decided it's time to go?"

"This – this place—" I could barely get the words out. "God damn it, Miranda, someone mutilated you! They turned you into a – a—"

"A freak?" Lady Alligator tossed its head back and laughed again, louder this time. It was not a pleasant sound; it was the cackle of a witch in a fairy tale. "Oh, dear sweet Arthur. You of all people should know I've always been a freak. Different. You could read it on the faces of every person in that shithole town, I belonged there no more than a tiger belongs as a housecat."

I stood there, holding my jacket towards her like an idiot.

"Yes, someone did this to me, if that's how you want to put it. They plucked me from the crowd that day in New York and they stripped my old life away from me like the thick layer of country dirt that it was." It ran its palms along the mottled skin of its arms, tenderly, as though remembering when the flesh had been smooth and perfect. "A little gasoline and a flame, that's all it took."

"Miranda," I said, because I thought maybe saying her name again would bring her back to me, "I thought you left. I thought you left me at that intersection, you're saying someone took you?"

"Poor Arthur." I had the feeling it was repeating my name, too, but for a different reason. Lady Alligator regarded me with quiet distaste. "It happens in the city all the time. Women are taken. Sometimes for sex shows, sometimes for... other reasons." It gestured vaguely to the amber glow of its tiny trailer room.

"You didn't leave me," I said. My voice sounded strangely flat. The smell of sex and shit wafted past me again and I tried not to breathe it in.

"We all leave in different ways." Lady Alligator pursed its lips as if in thought. "If you're asking did I leave you at that intersection? No. I was taken, like I told you."

Before I could even let this sink in it went on.

"I had been planning to leave, though, if that makes any difference," it said, that terrible grin splitting its mouth, all those sharpened teeth glittering in the candlelight. "Surely you noticed my jewelry was gone. And the money. You thought you'd been so clever, dear Arthur, but you're as predictable as you are boring, and I knew it would be in the Bible in the drawer."

I had been right all along. I had been wrong but somehow I had been right.

"I wanted to get lunch, first. I thought the least you could do was feed me before I went," Lady Alligator mused, then laughed again. The sound echoed off the tin walls and vibrated in my skull.

I looked at its skin, the destroyed web of burnt tissue that covered it like a grotesque lace veil, and thought, *How poetic*. My wife had finally let the flame inside consume her.

I still held the coat out towards it.

"Did you ever love me?" I asked, and I knew I sounded as pathetic as the dull Nebraskan boy she'd always considered me to be.

The monster Miranda had become pressed its lips together and favored me with a tight smile. I thought for one wild moment it was going to say something kind.

"Oh, Arthur," Lady Alligator murmured. "Can an eagle love a worm? Can the brilliant sun love a dirty light bulb in a truckstop bathroom? Darling, you've always known that you captured me like a firefly in a jar. You thought if you didn't poke holes in the lid I'd be content to suffocate in your sweaty grasp but you dropped the glass and I escaped. And now I'm where I was always meant to be."

It said this with the deliberate patience of a mother explaining something to an especially dimwitted child. I felt it, then – the anger that had roiled my guts when I opened the drawer and saw the money missing from the Gideon Bible. Not because she'd robbed me, but because she'd deceived me. She made me believe she loved me and she left me and I grieved for her, god damn it, I grieved in my own way as though I'd been made a widower and the whole fucking time she was laughing at me.

"I bring in thousands," it went on. "They come from all corners of the world to see me. I'm the star attraction here. I can have any man I want."

You're a selfish whoremonster in a dirty bathtub, I thought, but I didn't say anything.

Miranda's eyes, a shade of alien gold in the flickering glow of lit candles, squinted at me.

"You're just the same as you've always been," it said, a lilt of disappointment in its voice. "Such a terrible bore."

I put my suit jacket back on. Lady Alligator sighed deeply.

"Is this about the money?" It shifted in the tub and for a moment I saw the dark, destroyed flesh of what had once been its nipples. "I have money. You tell Buddy outside to give you $300 from my account. He'll take care of you and then we'll be square, all right, Arthur?"

Square?

"You know what," Lady Alligator said with a preening little tilt of its grotesque head, "tell him to throw in an extra hundred, a gift from me to—"

And then my hands were around its throat, the skin beneath my palms felt dry and scaly but I ignored it and squeezed tighter, relishing how Miranda's eyes widened in shock, drinking in the sound of its self-righteous voice finally silenced.

I thought I could save her.

Lady Alligator made a strangled noise as I took one hand away from its neck to shove its head beneath the grimy water. A great burst of bubbles erupted when I did but I threaded my fingers through its hair and gave it no leverage. I pushed down harder.

Its arms flailed helplessly. Its feet kicked. Its toes were painted red.

We remember the strangest things.

I held it underwater until it stopped moving. The mottled hands went limp and fell back into the tub. When I released it at last, it floated there like scum on a pond.

I'm not sure how long I stared at its body before reaching towards it, wanting to be sure it was dead, wanting to be sure the nightmare was truly over. I took it by its scaly shoulders and leaned it against the porcelain back of the bathtub. I brushed the hair from its face, just like I used to do when my wife was sleeping.

The mouth gaped in a wide, terrible smile. The pointed teeth gleamed. The destroyed skin shimmered in the candlelight.

Above the slit nose Miranda's eyes stared at me, blank.

A monster hidden in a dark room. That's who my wife was, and always had been.

I left New York that afternoon. Stumbled down the steps past Buddy the comic book reader in his booth and made my way to the nearest highway. I hitched a ride and never looked back.

You may think this was what spurred me on, encouraged me to live every day as though it was my last, the fear of being caught for her murder. But things were different back then. She was a freak in a sideshow, she mattered to the police as much as garbage in the gutter. And the sideshow, well, they could always... recruit fresh talent. There was a new Lady Alligator around every corner.

The truth is – and yes, I promised you the truth – that I have pushed every day of my life to the very brink because, as I said, I understand what most people don't. Life is finite, whether you believe it or not. We only get so many spins.

And I know, in that same dark room inside myself, that when I run out of spins, I'll face her again. It.

I'll pay for my sins by staring into those eyes, the same ones that shed a single tear on the day we were wed, the ones above that terrible smile. When my life is over my hell will begin, all pointed teeth and scaly skin. If you're reading this now, I'm already gone, and it's already started.

Live every day to the fullest.
We all leave in different ways.

2

THE PROM QUEEN IS DEAD

And you're not.

It's that simple. She's dead, the beautiful blonde who literally gasped in surprise when the principal read her name, announcing that she'd won. Someone caught it on camera and in a week or so you were pointing at that gasp without touching the photo to tell someone else on the yearbook staff yep, that's it, put that one in the center of the layout. You picked it because it was the prettiest, the most palatable, and not because you knew her in any way. You didn't care if she'd be excited and gasp again when she saw she was the focus of the Prom 2004 spread. You heard she was nice but you didn't know her because you didn't run in that crowd, the crowd of the pretty and the palatable. You just knew the picture looked good in the center. Now, 11 years later, in hundreds of homes there's a yearbook with a page where a beautiful blonde girl gasps as a tiara is being handed to her. This beautiful blonde will gasp forever and at age 28 she put a needle in her arm and OD'd on heroin and it's just that simple: the prom queen is dead and you're not.

Before her it was a guy from the varsity tennis team. You didn't know him either but for some reason you have a video on your computer of him playing guitar for your friends. It's senior year, everyone is sitting on the ground around him singing a song by Sublime and you're filming and last spring he got sideswiped by a semi truck on his motorcycle.

There was another girl, someone big in drama club, one of those Anne Hathaway types with too many teeth and too much to say. She wasn't your friend but she acted like she was when she was running for student council. Ran right up to you at lunch and threw her arms around you in a hug, asked how your summer went, if you'd lost weight. In that moment you hated her, hated the way your name sounded in her mouth, but you bit the bullet and smiled back, knowing that after she got your vote she'd never remember your name again. They found her in her garage a few years ago with the car running after her husband ran off with one of his male coworkers.

Your ex-boyfriend, the bad one, he hung himself in his apartment in Portland sometime around 2009. Before he did it he tweeted "You forget that I win". You're not sure what that was about but he always had a flair for the dramatic and now your ex-boyfriend is dead along with the rest of them.

The year you graduated from college, some guy you did a scene with in elective theater class got crushed by a tree while hiking through the Pacific Northwest. The scene you did together was something about the woman's bathroom and a Stradivarius cello and he was killed by an act of God during his church-sponsored nature retreat, ha-fucking-ha on that one. You can't remember the name of the play but think it had the word "Flowers" in the title.

After your first semester in college your roommate – the one who moved out without ceremony or telling you where she was going but managed to take your hair dryer and your trash can – she moved in with her boyfriend. You learned that much on Facebook, but you didn't hear until almost two years later how he'd strangled her one night after a fight about meth. They'd been tweaking for days.

The prom queen is dead, and so is the guy who played guitar. The girl with too many teeth in her head and your least favorite ex-boyfriend. The guy you acted with one afternoon and the girl you lived with one semester.

You're friends with too many of them on social networks. Twitter profiles with one final tweet that echoes on forever. Facebook pages that become burial markers, interactive graveyards where people still stop by and post as though the long-gone person who smiles at them from their profile picture will get the message. "Miss you." "Love you." "Wish you were still here." It's an embarrassing, fruitless attempt to contact the dead, an online Ouija board with no one on the other end.

You act cavalier about it, about the people you've known who are now in the ground. You pretend it's not a big deal. Maybe you write snarky little thinkpieces about it, like this one. But the truth is, the ugly stinking truth at the rotten core of the matter, is that it scares the shit out of you. The sheer number of people who were HERE and now just AREN'T. How fast it can happen, like a lightbulb going out. Sometimes it keeps you awake at night.

The prom queen, she had kids. Two of them. A boy and a girl who are barely out of diapers and now they'll grow up without that beautiful smiling blonde who, according to her Facebook profile, went on smiling long after the tiara was placed on her head, probably kept smiling right up until sticking the needle in her arm. The guy who played guitar for your friends, all of them beaming and singing "What I Got" at his feet, he had a wife and they were planning on starting a family that summer.

The girl from drama club, you didn't like her but she gave a monologue from "The Crucible" that took your breath away. Your ex-boyfriend was a piece of shit, sure, but there were plenty of times he made you laugh, made you feel good, and that's got to count for something.

The guy in the Pacific Northwest was there to help people. He had powerful faith in God, something that everyone praised for weeks after he died but how can you say that and ignore the fact that he was killed in the most unfair way? That he was struck down, literally, while doing God's work. Where was God then?

Your college roommate was sad. You could tell that from day one, her eagerness to be friends, her dark eyes that begged you (or anyone, really) to love her. Maybe if she'd met someone else, found a different guy to give herself to, she wouldn't have died on that dirty flophouse floor with his hands around her throat.

It's the fragility, the finality of it that terrifies you. How easy it can be to be gone forever. How easy it could be to be forgotten.

Because that's the root of it, isn't it? Death itself, that's not enough to shake you to your core because you imagine it's a lot like a dreamless sleep or how it was before you were born. What really scares you isn't the unending darkness you're pretty sure follows death. It's the idea of your funeral with few people in attendance. It's the people you love unable to remember your face clearly. It's your Facebook page, a barren wasteland, no one stopping by to say they miss you.

It's being forgotten.

And sure, you haven't forgotten. Even the people you didn't really know, they occupy a small slice of your mind. The guy plays his guitar for your singing friends and your shitty ex-boyfriend tells you he prefers brunettes to blondes so you consider dyeing your hair. Your former roommate writes "hi cuteface" on the dry erase board of your shared dorm. The girl who reminds you of Anne Hathaway insists she's a good girl, a proper girl. Your acting partner makes too many jokes while you're trying to rehearse so you spend most of the time laughing and can't remember your lines. The blonde smiles, smiles, smiles.

But you. What makes you special enough to be remembered?

You sat down to write a horror story and you've found out what really scares you instead.

But the important thing to remember, I suppose, is this:

The prom queen is dead and you're not.

3

GOT TO GIVE

The woman wearing sunglasses looked furtively left down the empty street, then right, as though she were afraid of being followed. Shivering like a scared puppy, even in the warm California weather. Plucking nervously at the scarf that covered her head.

The wooden sign that hung on the brick before her promised in faded black letters: PAST! PRESENT! FUTURE! In a smaller, curlier style below, it read: *crystal ball gazing, palm reading, tarot cards.* Above all that, in grand sprawling glamour: MADAME ZARA. COME IN.

After a long hesitation and a mental pep-talk, she finally entered the fortune teller's shop.

Inside, it was dark and smelled faintly of the loose-rolled joints the delivery boys smoked on the curb of the corner store where she bought her weekly groceries — when she felt inclined to eat, of course. And always in disguise, always with the scarf to hide her brilliant hair, always behind large dark sunglasses. Never mind the heat.

With small, delicate steps she made her way past gauzy curtains and bronze statues of yawning dragons. The silence was suffocating.

She'd begun to think it was a trick, people were often out to make her feel foolish, stupider than she actually was; perhaps this was all part of their plot against her, to see if she was dumb enough to really fall for a fortune teller's lure, tears were welling hot behind the sunglasses and she was ready to turn around and flee when she heard:

"Seet down, my lovely. Seet down, right there, I have been vaitink for you."

The woman took the sunglasses off with a pale, shaking hand. The room became brighter, but not by much, though now she could see the shadowy figure seated behind a round table at the rear of the shop. It was gesturing towards her.

"I — I'm dreadfully sorry," she said, her voice breathy. "I didn't — didn't see you there, the glasses, I think—" Even as she said this her fingers played nervously along the sunglasses she'd removed, like she yearned to put them back on.

"Seet," the shadow said again.

She hesitated. Looked back towards the entrance. Finally, chewing nervously at her bottom lip, she walked to the table and sat down.

"You were... waiting for me?"

The shadow wasn't a shadow at all, but a woman not much older than she was. Thick, dark hair cascaded over her shoulders in waves. She had hard features and a hooked nose yet still didn't look quite like the witch the woman in the head scarf had expected.

The fortune teller gestured towards her again with fingers stacked with jeweled rings. They glinted in the low light like fireflies.

"Seet," she said.

The woman sat.

The fortune teller regarded her solemnly over a crystal ball, a beautiful perfect orb of glass that sat between them on the table. A long moment of silence passed; the woman opened her mouth to speak, unable to bear the heaviness of it, when the fortune teller spoke instead.

"Vat is your name, my lovely?" she asked. Her accent reminded the woman of Boris Karloff as Dracula.

"Zelda," the woman said tentatively. "Zelda Zonk, pleased to meet you."

"Ahh, but vat a coincidence!" The fortune teller folded her bejeweled fingers together, amused. "My name, as you may have seen from the sign, is Madame Zara. Zelda and Zara, ve verr destined to meet today."

"Were we?" the woman said, placing her sunglasses and pocketbook on the table. In the crystal ball, their faces were warped like a funhouse mirror.

"Yeeeeessss." Madame Zara drew out the word, long and low, the hiss of a snake. "As I said, I have been vaitink for you." She spread her hands out, a graceful gesture; the woman marveled at the fortune teller's long sharp nails, lacquered shiny and red as blood. "Vat are you here for, my lovely Zelda Zonk?"

I thought you could see the future, the woman thought, but bit back the urge to say.

"I'm — I'm not sure it's — a service you offer," she murmured, plucking at the scarf that covered her hair.

Madame Zara's lips spread in a smile. "Do you wish for me to read your palms?"

Before she could answer, the fortune teller shook her head.

"No, that is not it. Shall I gaze into my crystal ball and tell your fortune?"

"I'm afraid I already know what the future holds for me," the woman said quietly.

Madame Zara let loose a barking laugh that made the woman start in her seat.

"As so many beautiful ladies do!" she cried, delighted. "Oh, my lovely Zelda, you are not here for tea leaves or tarot cards or the alignment of the stars. I have been playink vith you, darlink, I know exactly vy you are here."

The woman stared at her in wonder.

"Why?" she breathed.

"You are looking," Madame Zara said, leaning over her crystal ball, "for an answer to a problem."

Another silence passed between them. Then the woman nodded.

"Yes. Do you have my answer, Madame Zara?" Her hands twisted together tightly in her lap like rodents in combat.

The fortune teller's smile faded to a thin smirk.

"Maybe I do, darlink," she said, and when she spoke next her voice was suddenly devoid of the syrupy vampire accent. "But first you'll have to be honest with me, Norma Jeane."

The woman sat there, stunned. Even her hands went still.

"I — I told you, m-my name is—"

"You told me a crock of shit." Madame Zara motioned at the scarf on the woman's head. "That may fool the general public, Miss *Monroe*, but the sight goes far beyond a silly piece of satin. Take it off."

The woman's mouth seemed to search for words before she gave up and untied the scarf, pulling it off with trembling hands. Even in the dim light of the fortune teller's shop, her platinum blonde hair gleamed brilliantly.

"How did you know?" she asked, almost childlike in her wonder.

"I put on a show for my regular clientele," Madame Zara said casually, "but the sight is very real. I could feel you from the moment you walked in. It radiates off you, Norma Jeane, like heat."

"What does?" Norma Jeane whispered. She was leaning towards the fortune teller, utterly enthralled.

"Rage." Madame Zara paused, then stood up from the table and moved quickly to the front of the shop. Norma Jeane turned to watch, the scarf fluttering from her lap unnoticed.

"What are you doing?"

Madame Zara flipped the plastic 'OPEN' sign hanging from the front door over to 'CLOSED' and rejoined her at the table.

"What we have to discuss," the fortune teller said, threading her fingers together so the glass jewels in her rings clicked against each other, "is not for the ears of outsiders."

Norma Jeane swallowed thickly.

"So you *do* know why I'm here."

Madame Zara regarded her with a stern, even gaze.

"Are you sure revenge is the way to go, sweetheart?" she asked, gentle, the way a teacher might speak to a wayward student. "Men of their type find their own wicked ends, one way or another."

The beautiful blonde's lips quivered, as though she were about to burst into tears, but instead she slammed her hands on the table in a sudden jerky movement. The crystal ball wobbled precariously on its stand.

"No, they don't!" she spat, all at once full of the fury the fortune teller had described. "They get away with it, they get away with it and get away with it and it's *not fair!*"

Madame Zara was unfazed. She placed the tip of one lacquered fingernail on the ball, stilling it.

"You want them to be held accountable?"

"I want them," Norma Jeane said through gritted teeth, "to fucking *pay.*"

The fortune teller chuckled.

"The studios certainly don't let you use *that* kind of language in your pictures, now do they?"

Norma Jeane clenched her fists.

"I have the money," she went on. "As much as you need. But it has to be good. I *need* it to be good. Powerful. Strong."

"Strong how?" Madame Zara was regarding her with a fresh kind of interest. This was not the same mousy woman who had entered her shop wearing sunglasses; this was someone *new*.

"I want them to suffer." Norma Jeane paused, considering this, then added, "I want their children to suffer. Their grandchildren. I want their whole goddamn bloodline *cursed.*"

The fortune teller let out a long, low whistle.

"That's a hefty thing you're asking for, Norma Jeane," she said. "The cost for something like this is high."

Instantly, Norma Jeane grabbed for her pocketbook.

"I already said, I've got plenty of money," she spat, clicking it open to reveal a fat wad of hundred dollar bills. She grabbed a handful and slammed it on the table. "How much? This much? I won't even count it."

Madame Zara's dark eyes flicked from the cash, to the blonde, back to the cash again. After a moment, she carefully selected seven crisp bills and pushed the rest back towards Norma Jeane.

"That settles your earthly debt," she murmured. "Now there's the darker part to consider."

Norma Jeane shook her head, not understanding, and reached for more money despite the stack of bills on the table.

"You can take it all—"

"Norma Jeane, it's not about money." The fortune teller was delicately folding her payment, tucking it away somewhere inside the gauzy fabric of her gypsy costume. "What you're asking for is black. It involves death, and tragedy, and blood."

The beautiful blonde's eyes shone with angry tears.

"I poured myself into that dress like a glass of cheap champagne," she whispered hotly, "for *him*. Then he wouldn't even take my calls! And his *brother*—" Her ample bosom was heaving as she struggled to get the words out. "—he pawned me off on his *brother* because that *cunt* of a wife of his was threatening to leave, and I was so *stupid* I fell for that too!" She rapped one knuckle hard against her shining platinum hair. It made an unpleasant thunking sound in the silence of the shop. "They both said, they said what they always say, what men always say — 'I love you, only you, you're the most beautiful woman in the world'—"

Another hard thump on her skull.

"—but they don't mean it!" At this, she let out a sudden yelping cry, the beginning of what might have been a sobbing fit had she not cut it off in time. Norma Jeane met eyes with the fortune teller as two perfect tears slid down her cheeks, pretty as a movie scene. "They *never* mean it," she whispered, and now she no longer sounded angry — just lost and sad, a scared child without her mother.

Madame Zara looked deep into her crystal ball, but it was more a show for Norma Jeane, something to calm her down, keep her focused.

"The soldier and the athlete," she murmured, waving her jeweled fingers over the ball, "the playwright and the politicians."

"I hate them all," Norma Jeane said, broken. "But the brothers most. Because to them it was a game. At least with the others, they *tried*."

Madame Zara gave her a long, hard look.

"You want them to suffer," she echoed.

"Their whole goddamn bloodline," Norma Jeane repeated firmly.

The fortune teller paused, testing the waters, drawing out the silence, waiting to see if the blonde would change her mind.

She didn't. It was a standoff that Norma Jeane won. And so Madame Zara told her the price.

"Men take," she said softly. "This, you know. Men take and women give. For something like this, you've got to give a *lot*."

Norma Jeane nodded.

"Anything."

The fortune teller licked her lips, then gestured towards Norma Jeane.

"What you carry inside," Madame Zara said.

The blonde sat there for a moment, unable to comprehend what she meant. Then it hit her.

"Am — am I—" She clasped her hands over her midsection, twisting the fabric of her dress. "No, not that, please. Anything else. I can give you anything else."

"I don't make the rules, sweetheart," Madame Zara explained, grimacing. "He does. I told you, men take, and He's the one who sets the price. If you offer Him your sacrifice, you'll get what you want, it's that simple. Blood for blood."

"I've lost so many of them," Norma Jeane whimpered. "Can't I keep just one? Please? *Anything* else?" Clutching her stomach tightly.

Madame Zara made a gesture with her jeweled hands, suggesting that the matter was out of them.

"You give, you get your revenge. You don't, you leave. These are the choices." She paused, then added hastily, "No cash refunds, by the way."

Norma Jeane chewed furiously at her lower lip.

"I need to think."

"You said you've lost them," the fortune teller offered. "Who's to say you won't lose this one too? And with it, your chance to make them pay?"

The idea was tempting. Norma Jeane turned it over in her brain, slowly, again and again.

Blood for blood.

"You have the sight," Norma Jeane said at last. "Can you tell me if I'll lose my baby again? Or not? Can you help me?"

But Madame Zara already knew the answer to this. She had already seen how it would play out before the movie star ever walked into her darkened shop.

"You will lose it," she said flatly.

A quiet little gasp escaped Norma Jeane, but already she was nodding, hands still grasping her stomach as if she could protect the unborn baby inside.

"All right, then," she breathed. Nodding harder and harder. "All right, then, all right. I'll do it. He can have it. Just make it happen. The brothers. Their bloodline. I want it poisoned from now until eternity."

So it was done.

Madame Zara crossed one palm over the other. She placed them towards Norma Jeane, over her heart, at the core of her being. She closed her eyes.

Norma Jeane felt something inside slip, like when you take a step only to find you've missed one stair. Like the bottom was dropping out. Or perhaps she only imagined that she felt something.

The fortune teller opened her eyes.

"It has been cast," she said, and she sounded strangely tired.

"That's all?" Norma Jeane asked in a small, childlike voice. Madame Zara nodded.

"That's all. It will happen in time." Then, for the first time, she told Norma Jeane a lie: "You will see it."

The blonde nodded, and to the fortune teller's surprise, burst into tears.

"I should feel better, I know," she confessed, wiping harshly at her eyes with the heel of her palm, "but right now I'm just... sad. And broken." Norma Jeane looked up at Madame Zara, forcing a smile that was beautiful even in her sorry state. "I just wanted them to love me."

The fortune teller stared at her, the gorgeous actress, one of the biggest stars in the world, the woman loved by everyone and no one at the same time, the sad fragile specimen who within the week would be found dead and alone and all the headlines would read was that she was naked when it happened.

Madame Zara said, "Go home, Norma Jeane."

With shaking hands, the blonde collected her things from the table. She retrieved the scarf from the floor, tied it around her hair again, replaced her sunglasses. She made her way to the front door, clutching her pocketbook tightly. She was almost outside when she paused, turning back just a bit to look at the fortune teller.

"When I was a little girl," Norma Jeane said, her tone wavering, "I saw a stray dog dragging something into an alley. I thought it was a cat, you see, so I followed it, thinking maybe I could help. But it wasn't a cat. It was one of those organ grinder monkeys. He was wearing a little hat, a little vest. He was screaming."

She let out a humorless laugh.

"I wish someone had told me Hollywood was like that."

Madame Zara began to slowly take off each of her rings, one by one, lining them up next to each other on the table and trying to push away the image of Norma Jeane cold and stiff, facedown in her bed. The jewels were beautiful but they made her hands hurt.

"Sweetheart," the fortune teller said, "that's not Hollywood. That's life."

4

TRACKING

___

BALLET RECITAL 1992

The first DVD arrived in my mailbox on Thursday, April 11 2013. I remember because it had been rainy, one of those gross squishy spring days where your shoes stick in the mud that seems to be everywhere. My mailbox had leaked, making most of the mail inside soggy and damp — but not the slim, clear plastic DVD case stuck between weekly pennysavers and credit card offers.

It wasn't in an envelope. It didn't have a postmark or a stamp or even an address. It must've just been... left there.

In bold Sharpie-black letters, the disk read: BALLET RECITAL 1992.

My first thought, naive as it was, was that Mom had probably dropped it off. Like, maybe she'd been converting some old home movies and wanted to surprise me. Seems so stupid now. I should've just thrown it away. Instead, I dumped the rest of the wet mail into the trash and slipped the DVD into my MacBook.

It was Thursday, April 11 2013 that everything changed.

The footage started normal enough. Living up to the title written so neatly on the disk, I found myself watching a tiny version of me — little Amanda Schneider in ballet flats and a puffy pink tutu, twirling aimlessly around a stage with other 6-year-olds who twirled with the same childish aimlessness. Those white lines that used to come up on VHS videos with bad tracking crept in and out of the recital. They brought back a strange sense of nostalgia.

I was just picking up my phone to call Mom and thank her for my gift when the footage suddenly cut out.

In a dark room, lit ruthlessly in the face by some off-screen source, sat a woman. She was wearing a ballet outfit, tutu and all — not unlike the one I wore in my recital video. On top of her head was a mussed ballerina bun, sadly askew. Her cheeks were covered in almost equal measure with third-degree burn scars and streaky smudged mascara. Over her mouth was a thick strip of duct tape.

Had it not been for the burn scars I might not've recognized her. But I did. That, and her eye — the one that was squinched almost closed, swollen from the burns — I could never have forgotten that eye.

It was my childhood best friend, Gretchen. Gretchen Hartman.

"Oh my god," I said to no one in particular. It had been years, probably 9 or 10, since I'd seen her. Probably nearly that long since she'd even crossed my mind.

Tears leaked from Gretchen's eyes, the normal one and the disfigured one. She kept shaking her head, looking off-camera at someone. Or some*thing*.

Have you ever seen something so unbelievable, so unexpected, that it doesn't seem real? One time, when I was a kid, I saw a terrible accident. It happened right in front of me and I couldn't look away but I couldn't do anything to help, either. This felt like that.

Gretchen let out a wail from behind the duct tape and squeezed her eyes closed. She shook her head harder. Her shoulders strained helplessly against what could only be very tight bonds. I heard my heartbeat pounding thick in my ears.

Suddenly, Gretchen's eyes popped wide open — like maybe she was in pain or something — and the footage cut off her following scream, going immediately to black.

I sat there for a long moment, dumbstruck. Then, across the screen in tall white letters standing out against the black like bones in tar:

INVOLVE THE POLICE AND SHE DIES

These hovered before me, then:

WAIT FOR MORE

And then it was over.

I stared at my MacBook. The video player stared back. With shaking fingers I clicked the play icon. I watched as the footage started over again: me in my innocent little ballerina outfit, Gretchen's burnt skin, the bun askew on her head, the duct tape over her mouth. The squinted, squashed eye. The warning at the end: *involve the police and she dies.*

Of everything I'd seen in the video, that was the easiest to understand.

My hand hovered over my iPhone anyway. How would whoever had sent the DVD know whether I had called the police? Well, that was simple enough: they knew where I lived. That was obvious. The DVD hadn't been mailed to my house, it had been placed in the mailbox, like a horrible little present.

Why me? And why, of all people, Gretchen?

While I sat there, MacBook glowing in the low light of that dreary April day, I found myself doing something I hadn't done in a long time: thinking about my childhood. There's a good reason for that, too. I avoided thinking about my childhood because we tend to avoid things with teeth, and my memories of growing up had just that — dark spots, black places, and gleaming in those shadows, long sharp teeth.

I met Gretchen when I was six years old, about three months after the ballet recital on the DVD. Dad had lingered in the hospital choking on his own blood for as long as I could remember; when he died, we couldn't afford payments on the nice little brick house in Suburbia so a few days after the funeral Mom packed us up and off we went. I was pretty young but I remember thinking, why so fast? Why now? Why did I have to lose my dad AND my house, my school, my friends — all in the same summer?

When you're an adult you can put some perspective on the situation. Mom was always a proud lady, our funds had been drained with Dad in the ICU for so long and she couldn't bear a foreclosure on top of everything else.

I still think it was a shitty thing to do to a kid.

We took what Mom hadn't sold and moved into low-income housing in what I'd heard called "The Bad Part Of Town," all ominous and worthy of capital letters. We pulled up in front of it, a squat little yellow tinderbox half the size of our pretty gingerbread house with the sturdy columns and stained glass windows. Two square windows on either side of a door that seemed to me like eyes and a mouth, calling out, "Come in, Amanda. I'm hungry. I want to eat you up just like cancer ate your Daddy up from the inside."

The first day we were there, I couldn't stop crying. I tried, I really did, but I couldn't and Mom yelled that I was useless but I knew she was just upset about Dad so I went to sit on the crumbly cement step out front to let her unpack the kitchen in peace.

I rubbed at my eyes with the heels of my hands until I saw stars exploding in the darkness. It hurt, but also felt kinda good too, so I kept doing it even though Mom had said before that I shouldn't.

"My mommy says that's bad for your eyes," said someone behind the exploding stars.

I stopped and looked up to see another girl, a girl my age with kinky red hair and thick cokebottle glasses. They had pink rims and I remember the color looked weird with her hair.

"Why?" I sniffled, trying not to let on that I was crying even though it was obvious I had been. "Is that what happened to you?"

The girl shrugged, but said, "No. I woke up one day and couldn't see Tom and Jerry very good on the TV and my mommy took me to the doctor and they said I gots near-sights."

"Oh," I said, assuming that meant she had almost-sight and accepting it as fact.

"Why you cryin'?" Gretchen squinted at me. She didn't have the burn scars yet or the scrunched up eye, just lots and lots of freckles.

I didn't really want to tell this red-haired girl with glasses that my life as I knew it was over, but for some reason I found myself saying, "my dad died," wiping tears from my cheeks. I'd finally stopped crying. "He was sick for a long time and now we're poor so we live here."

An adult might've taken that as an insult but Gretchen's face lit up.

"I'm poor too!" she exclaimed brightly, clasping her hands together. "Most everyone 'round here is! But not a lot of kids. 'Specially not girls. We could be friends!"

I sniffed again. Looked her over with the frank, unbiased consideration only children are afforded. Seemed to come up with one answer: my friends were gone, Mom was mad all the time, and even though Gretchen wasn't much, this one would have to do.

"Okay," I said, with not as much enthusiasm as I think she'd expected. Her face clouded over a little, eyes growing dark behind those thick glasses. Eager to get her good mood back — I'd had enough bad moods with Mom, as it were — I added, "I have a Lisa Frank friendship bracelet kit inside. You want me to go get it?"

Her smile returned, brighter than ever.

"Yep yep yep!" Gretchen chirped, reminding me of Ducky from *The Land Before Time*. Ducky's my favorite, so suddenly I felt a little better. Better than I had in a while.

"Can I call you Ducky?" I asked shyly, unsure if this was reaching too far for a new friend. Gretchen flushed pink under her freckles, matching the rims of her glasses, and gave me a hard brief hug.

"I never had a nickname before," she said. "Yep yep yep, I'll be your Ducky, let's make bracelets!"

And we did.

I heeded the DVD's warning and didn't call the cops. After a night of sleep, I still wasn't sure what I was supposed to do. Gretchen and I hadn't spoken in years, I wasn't even friends with her on Facebook and didn't have her family's contact information. I considered calling Mom but I didn't really want her involved in this either.

I was holding my iPhone in one sweaty palm, going over my options the way my grandmother used to worry over a small smooth stone with an imprint for her thumb, when it occurred to me.

WAIT FOR MORE.

I ran out to the mailbox even though I knew the chain-smoking mailman wouldn't be around for another few hours and was less than surprised to see another slim, clear plastic case resting inside — docile yet dangerous, like a coiled cobra with poison fangs.

I pulled it out and cringed when I read what was printed on it, the same blocky permanent-marker print: SOFTBALL GAME 1995

Shit.

This was only going to get worse.

SOFTBALL GAME 1995

The permanent-marker words taunted me from the shiny surface of the DVD. I'd been staring at it for half an hour, chewing at my acrylic thumbnail, too scared to put it in my MacBook but unwilling to throw it away. What was on this DVD was bound to be worse than the last one.

I had three options: 1) throw the DVD away and leave Gretchen to her fate, 2) call the cops and possibly be responsible for her death, 3) watch the DVD and go from there.

I sighed. Put the DVD in my laptop. Held my breath.

The opening footage was shaky, focused on 9-year-old me, growing girl Amanda Schneider at bat during a sweaty summer softball game. Knobby knees, awkward elbows. My favorite beat-up LA Dodgers hat on my head. I watched as I looked over my shoulder, unsure, towards the camera in the stands.

"Don't look at me, Mandy, look at the pitcher!" a deep, masculine voice boomed. I covered my face with my hands, knowing what was coming, but peeked through my fingers.

Nine-year-old me glanced back towards the mound just a hair too late; the softball zoomed past without a swing.

"Oh, Jesus H. Christ," the voice came again.

Shut up, I thought bitterly. *Shut up, shut up. I'm just a kid.*

"Strike one," called the umpire.

"Get your goddamn head in the game, Mandy," the man yelled. Nine-year-old me's shoulders slumped but I didn't turn around.

It was useless, I remember thinking. That girl was an incredible pitcher. There was a rumor that her dad iced her arm every night.

The next pitch was a fireball; I swung hard but the ball hit the catcher's mitt with a crack. Strike two.

"What did we practice for all week, Mandy?"

I hated those practices. I hated softball, too, after a while.

The pitcher wound up, rocketed another screamer across the plate. I swung, tipped off the ball. The catcher caught it, no sweat.

"Fuckin' typical," said my step-dad, and lowered the camera just as it cut to Gretchen again.

She was in the same dark room, same harsh light on her pale face. Freckles and scar tissue stuck out in brilliant contrast. Cockeyed on her head was a faded blue hat with the iconic interconnected L and A — I was shocked to realize it was the hat, the same hat from the video, the favorite hat I thought I lost when I moved out of that awful yellow house for good.

She was weeping, mouth still covered with duct tape. It looked fresh. Her hair, once bright red and kinky, hung limp in her face. It was the color of old rust.

Gretchen leaned forward, sagging against her bonds. She looked exhausted. My hat teetered on her head but didn't fall.

The next two minutes were just of her sobbing quietly into the duct tape.

Then, cut to black —

JOGGING ANY MEMORIES?

A pause, then —

FIGURE IT OUT. WAIT FOR MORE. NO COPS

Then —

OR SHE DIES

I didn't bother to watch the video a second time. I was already thinking about that summer of 1995, the one where I told Gretchen about my stepdad and how he was making my life a living hell.

"He yells at my softball games," I said glumly, picking at a loose thread on my comforter.

"A lot of parents do that." Gretchen was thumbing through one of my *Tiger Beats*, pausing to take a closer look at Mario Lopez shirtless. "It's supposed to hype you up."

"Yeah, but that's not what he's doing. Clay doesn't yell nice things, he yells mean stuff." I pulled on the thread and watched as it unraveled. I wondered how I was going to get out of next week's game.

"Like what?" she asked, only half-interested. Mario Lopez's abs were more appealing than my problems for the moment.

"He makes fun of me. Tells me I should be doing better. We practice all week, Gretchen, the whole stupid week but as soon as I get up to bat I get all... watery."

Gretchen lowered the magazine and regarded me from behind her thick lenses. She'd gotten new frames, silver wire instead of pink. They suited her, made her look kind of like a librarian. A smart one, not a mean one.

"Watery?"

"Yeah," I said, seeing how far I could pull the loose thread before it broke. "Like, in my legs. I don't know how to stand or when to swing even though I really do. I can just feel him up in the stands with that god damn camera, watching me."

She ignored my rare use of a curse word and set the magazine down.

"I'm sorry. That really sucks."

"It does," I agreed. My fingers plucked at the string for another moment, then I let it go and looked at Gretchen. "I don't know what my mom sees in him. He's gross. And mean. And not like..." I trailed off, unwilling to say it, but Gretchen knew what I meant.

"He's nothing like your dad," she said gently, putting a hand on my knee. "From what you told me, I can tell that right off."

I forced a smile and rested my hand on hers.

"Thanks, Ducky. It's hard to explain but I knew you'd get it."

Gretchen squeezed my knee twice, one of our codes for "everything's going to be okay," then let it go and began leafing through *Tiger Beat* again in search of more cute boys.

"Why'd your mom marry Clay in the first place?"

"Nuts if I know," I muttered, reaching past her for another issue. "She says he's nice to her but I don't see it. Maybe it's just because he makes money."

"He doesn't make a lot or you wouldn't still be stuck here." Gretchen said this breezily but I could tell there was tension in her voice. We'd been best friends for three years, I knew when she was getting upset.

"I'm not stuck here, dummy. I'm glad I get to live near you."

There was a moment where Gretchen seemed to be staring not at the magazine but through it. Then she said, "One day, you won't be."

Before I could ask what she meant, Gretchen was tossing the magazine aside, swinging her freckled legs over the side of my bed and hopping down.

"C'mon. Let's go make some Jiffy Pop. I'm starved."

"Clay's out there," I said wearily, knowing he'd be two or three beers deep by this time of night.

"What's he gonna do?" She put her hands on her hips and jutted out her lower lip in that way she did when she got sassy. "I'll knock his teeth out if he says anything to you. Besides, you're not exactly at bat right now. You're just going to make your best friend in the world some popcorn. Let's see him heckle you at THAT."

That made me laugh. Gretchen could always make me laugh. So we did as she said and made some popcorn and wouldn't you know it, Clay didn't even look in our direction once.

There were no new clues in the footage to tell me where Gretchen was being held or if there was anything I could do other than recognize my Dodgers cap. And what did that mean? For all I knew, Mom had donated it to Goodwill when I left for college. I was left with nothing.

I couldn't do this alone.

After a few hours of thinking, I picked up my iPhone and jabbed out a text message to my best friend Erin:

Can you come over? I need your help with something. Don't tell anyone. It's super urgent.

I hesitated, then before I could talk myself out of it, hit send.

While I stared at my phone, waiting for Erin to reply, I thought about how I'd quit softball two weeks after that video had been shot. Clay had been furious; Mom was the only reason I wasn't forced to go back. For the rest of the summer, I hid in my room and tried to imagine what life would've been like if my dad hadn't gotten sick all those years ago.

Erin typed back:

Sure babe, on my way

I responded:

Thanks. Can you do me a favor and check the mailbox on your way in?

I ran to the door, nearly slipping on the hardwood in my socked feet. I opened it to see Erin. She was holding a new DVD case.

"Is this what you were looking for?" she asked, puzzled, and held it up towards me.

SCHOOL PLAY 1998

"Fuck," I said, and let her in.

<hr/>

SCHOOL PLAY 1998

It took me about an hour to explain everything to Erin. Well, not everything, if I'm being honest. I didn't tell her much about Gretchen, just that she had been a friend of mine when we were kids. I also didn't go into detail about Clay — just said he was a shitty step-dad and moved on.

At first she thought I was fucking with her. She had this look on her face like she was waiting for me to burst out laughing and say "Just kidding!" but that look went away when I played her the first DVD.

"Jesus Christ," Erin said, putting a hand over her mouth. She glanced from me, to the screen, back to me.

"Yeah," I agreed grimly.

She was silent, staring at the video until the final warning message flashed across the screen:

INVOLVE THE POLICE AND SHE DIES

"You have to do something, Amanda," Erin said at last. She'd gone pale; her skin was the color of rotten milk.

"I know. That's why I called you. I'm too scared to call the cops, even though that's all I can think of. Here, there's another one."

"There's ANOTHER one?" she echoed incredulously, and watched it play with the same stunned silence as the first.

When Clay began heckling me, she gave me this side-eyed glance that told me she felt sorry for me but didn't know what to say. I've seen that look enough to know exactly what it means.

When the second one was over, Erin held up the DVD she'd brought from the mailbox.

"So that means..."

"Yeah." I rubbed my hands over my face, not caring whether I smeared my winged eyeliner or not. "I'm scared to watch it, Erin."

"Me too," she said, but took it out of the case anyway. "We have to, though. You know that, right?"

"Yeah," I said again.

"Here." Erin handed me the disc that read SCHOOL PLAY 1998 and I slipped it into my MacBook. "You know what, you called me for help so I'm going to do whatever I can. Let's play Nancy Drew this time and really watch it for clues."

"Clues?" I asked, making the video player fullscreen. "Like what?"

"I don't know, something. Anything. Maybe there's some detail in here that will tell us where she is." She paused, then snapped her fingers like a detective in an old noir movie who's just realized his hunch. "The last one said figure it out! They WANT you to know... I don't know, but there's something they want you to 'figure out.' Right?"

"Okay, yeah, that makes sense." As much sense as this could make, anyway. I smiled and knuckle-bumped her on the shoulder. "That's why I called you, I knew you'd see this from a better angle than I could."

Erin grinned.

"Not a better one, just a different one. Come on, play this bitch."

I clicked play.

I already knew what to expect — I remembered what play I'd been in the year of 1998. That's why I didn't let out a shocked burst of laughter like Erin did.

Don't think she's mean or anything — I would've laughed, too, if I hadn't known what was coming.

The opening footage showed a small stage set up in a middle school cafeteria. Beyond it, you could see the shuttered kitchen full of supplies, pots, pans. This did little to help the forced environment onstage; a sadly decorated Christmas tree flanked either side and between them were a motley crew of characters — tweens dressed up in bright colors, some wearing wings — but at stage center stood a short guy who'd clearly not hit puberty yet, covered from head to toe in black fur. He wore floppy dog ears and a bright red collar. At his left was a girl who looked like Dolly Parton carrying a magic wand.

And there I was: blue-checked dress, curled hair in pigtails, glittery red shoes, wide ingenue eyes. In a cheerily false, projected voice 12-year-old-me said, "That's right Toto, back to Kansas! Because there's no place like home for the spirit of Christmas."

No place like home. What a joke.

"It's 'Christmas in the Land of Oz,'" I told Erin, feeling my cheeks burn.

"It's cute," she offered.

"It's fucking stupid is what it is."

The cast gathered together in an awkward, messy excuse for a group hug, then straightened out again for curtain call. That was it — that was the big finale for the cheap, cheesy excuse of a play. A tacked-on line from the classic film mashed together with some drivel about Christmas spirit. Bullshit.

If you hadn't seen this before, you would've missed the part where my real smile faltered and nearly disappeared when I spotted the camera in the audience. It was only a moment, a brief flicker across my face, but 12-year-old-me corrected quickly and went back to soaking up the applause with grace.

The footage cut to Gretchen like I knew it would. She was dressed up like Dorothy — like me. Her rust-red hair had been pathetically put into pigtails decorated with little blue ribbons. She was wearing a blue-checked dress, a cheap one that looked like it came from a Halloween shop. If I had to guess, she was probably wearing ruby slippers too, but I couldn't see her feet.

Another strip of fresh duct tape. I wondered briefly where her glasses had gone; she hadn't been wearing them in any of the videos. Did her kidnapper take them from her? Did she wear contacts now? Was this a clue, like Erin had said?

The video stopped, freezing Gretchen in a pose where she was staring miserably at whoever was behind the camera.

I began to panic, wondering if the footage had been corrupted, and saw that Erin had paused it.

"What are you doing?" I demanded frantically.

She held up one manicured hand. Erin was staring hard at the screen.

"Just look for a minute. Study everything. We can't see much, but there might be something here."

I had this crawly feeling, like I just wanted to watch the video and get it over with, but I leaned forward and looked too.

It was just a dark room, a stupid dark room with nothing in it, only the light and the chair and Gretchen. And, of course, the camera.

"I don't see—" I began, then stopped.

Behind her, barely visible, was wallpaper. That was it, it had to be wallpaper — it was this dirty gold color with splotches of brown and pea-soup green.

"What—" Erin said, but I waved a hand at her to shush. I leaned closer to the screen.

When I squinted, the splotches turned into flowers. Flowers being choked by winding leafy plants that were probably vines but... but...

"They looked like weeds," I whispered, and all at once my breakfast was in my throat.

I knocked over my office chair getting to the bathroom. I barely made it to the sink before the contents of my stomach burst out of me in a hot vile rush.

I could hear Erin in the other room, calling my name and coming after me, but she sounded a million miles away. I had forgotten. I had forgotten about the wallpaper and now I remembered, but only pieces, jagged little shards of memories that didn't fit together quite right.

Clay drove me home after the play. Mom was working but she saw the first half and that was okay because the play was pretty dumb anyway.

"You did a good job up there, Mandy," he said, not taking his eyes off the road. It was the first nice thing he'd said to me since... since I couldn't remember when.

"Thanks," I said, staring out the window glumly. I was back in my school clothes and parka but I'd kept the curled pigtails because they made me feel pretty, like Judy Garland in the real movie about Oz. I traced mindless patterns in the frost on the car window.

"I... I know I give you a hard time." Clay still wouldn't look at me but his voice got softer somehow so I chanced a glance at him out of the corner of my eye. "I was mad when you quit softball because I knew you could do better, that's all."

I didn't say anything. Waited for him to go on.

"But tonight, up there..." He let out a low whistle between his teeth. "You were great, Mandy, you really were. You..." Clay drifted off again, then looked at me and favored me with a rare smile. "You shine."

My chest felt hot and tight. I offered a small smile back.

"Thanks, Clay," I said shyly. His good nature was so unfamiliar to me I wasn't quite sure what to do; I sort of expected it to be like when a cat rolls on its back, offering you its tummy to pet, then scratches the shit out of you.

But he didn't say anything else. Just went through the Dairy Queen drive-thru and ordered me a cherry slushie, my favorite. I hadn't even known he knew it was my favorite.

When we got home, Clay stayed silent. He took the video camera in its bulky carrying case inside and I followed, wondering if it would be out of line to ask if I could watch the footage of the play tonight. I decided against it. Christmas vacation was almost there and I could watch it when Mom and Clay were at work.

He was settled in his armchair watching "Married With Children" reruns, a freshly opened beer in his hand, when I poked my head into the living room.

"I'm gonna take a shower and go to bed," I said quietly, trying not to drown out Al Bundy. "I'll see you tomorrow."

Clay grunted, noncommittal.

I paused, then added, "Thanks for coming to my play, Clay. It was nice of you."

He didn't respond. I took that as a win and padded my way to the bathroom, locking the door behind me.

The girl in the mirror stared back like she wasn't sure who I was. I suppose I wasn't sure who she was, either. Our director Mrs. Derst had applied all of our makeup before the show and, me being the lead, had taken the most time on mine. I hadn't worn makeup before, not for real, just when Gretchen and I were playing around with those fake sets we got for our birthdays. This was how makeup was supposed to look — how ladies looked on the covers of Mom's *Cosmopolitans*.

I turned my head to the side, admiring how mascara lengthened my lashes. I pursed my lips together. Red, like Dorothy wore in the movie. It looked nice but also kind of dirty, like mouths weren't supposed to look this vibrant, this showy. It was suddenly evident how much baby fat I'd lost in the last year or so.

As I tugged off my school clothes I thought about how I hoped I'd be pretty when I grew up. I knew Gretchen probably wouldn't be, as much as I loved her — she just had all those freckles and frizzy red hair and glasses that made her eyes look tiny in her head. I wished that Gretchen would turn out pretty too but little girls are selfish and most of all I wished it for me.

If I hadn't been so deep in thought, maybe I would've heard the click at the doorknob. The sound of the lock being disengaged. The quiet *woosh* of the door opening.

"I told you that you shine," Clay said softly.

I turned, covering my private areas with my hands, trying to shield my budding breasts from his view.

"You... you can't be in here!" I yelped.

He took another step towards me. Closed the door behind him.

Locked it.

I backed against the wall next to the toilet. I had nowhere else to go.

"You can't be in here," I said again, weakly, but he was moving towards me and all I could do was turn away, press my face against the vine-and-flower wallpaper, and in the last moments of my innocence I realized that the vines entwined around the flowers weren't vines at all... they just looked like weeds.

Erin was holding my hair back as I bent over the sink, retching. Saying soothing words into my ear. I was drenched in sweat.

I didn't speak for a long time. But when I did, I said through a mouth that tasted like vomit, "I know where she is."

ACCIDENT 1999

Erin stared at me, wide-eyed, still holding my hair back.

"You know where Gretchen is?" she said. I nodded and wiped my lips with the back of my hand. My mouth was full of that acidic sour-sick taste.

"Yeah." I turned the tap of the sink and ran cold water. Sipped delicately at it, rinsed, spit.

"Okay, I know you're clearly going through a thing right now but you can't leave me hanging like this," Erin said, sounding panicked.

I rinsed and spit again before turning to her.

"She's in my old house. The one on Turner Street. They've been filming in the bathroom."

"Is that what you saw?" she asked.

"Yeah. I recognized the wallpaper." Sure I did, I'd had my face pressed against it enough that I should've recognized it sooner. It was in that bathroom that Clay had raped me when I was 12, the first time after my school's Christmas play. How could I have forgotten? Dressed up like Dorothy, hair curled in perfect pigtails, smearing my grown-up mascara on the flowers and vines.

I never wore my hair in pigtails again but that hadn't stopped him.

"So let's go get her!" Erin exclaimed. I didn't respond right away; I chewed absently on one of my acrylic nails. "Amanda? Let's go get her, right?"

"We need to finish the video," I said, deciding not to tell her about Clay and the bathroom and why I recognized it.

"What?! Gretchen could be in serious trouble, we need to go get her and you know where she is so let's GO!" She gestured violently towards the door.

"You said it yourself," I said as I leaned away from the sink and headed back to the dining room where my MacBook waited on the table. "There's something they want us to figure out. I've got a piece but not all of it. We need to finish the video."

Erin stared at me like I was a crazy person then gave up, throwing her hands in the air.

"Okay, fine, but then we *gotta go!*"

We gathered around the screen. I wasn't sure if I could watch without getting sick again now that I knew where the videos were set but I had to try. I clicked play.

Gretchen jerked back to life, still watching whoever was behind the camera through miserable tears. She shook her head once, weakly. Her bad eye sagged, her burn marks lit in ruthless clarity.

Her irises flicked back and forth like her captor was pacing. Then it cut to black again —

YOU'RE ALMOST THERE

A beat, then —

DON'T GIVE UP YET

Then —

ONE MORE

And that was all.

"One more?" Erin said, puzzled.

"One more DVD." I swallowed against my sickly lurching stomach. "We can't do anything until that one shows up."

"Amanda, this is crazy!" She rewound the footage, found Gretchen's face again, then paused it and jabbed an accusing manicured finger at her. "Your friend is in serious trouble! If you really think we can't go to the cops but you know where she is — I mean, this could be a trick! What if they're just trying to stall you? By the time you finally show up after waiting for their last DVD — if there even is one — Gretchen could be dead!"

"That's not the game they're playing," I said softly. Something about this felt undeniable; there was a method to their madness. I was meant to remember something. I was meant to learn something.

Erin wouldn't understand. She hadn't been there.

We let a long, tense pause pass between us before I finally said, "Twenty-four hours. Okay? If I don't have anything in twenty-four hours, I'll just go to the house."

"Twenty-four hours—" Erin covered her face with her hands, overcome, then looked back at me. "Amanda, this isn't some Fox drama starring Kiefer Sutherland. It's not going to be wrapped up nice and pretty by the time the credits roll. This is a real person, a person you knew and cared about, and she could die."

"What the fuck am I supposed to do, Erin?" I demanded. "The video said to wait for one more! If I show up there before I see it, they might just kill her anyway! Or me! There's something here, something I'm missing, I need to find it! And it's on that last DVD!"

There was another moment of silence.

"What did you remember, Amanda?" she asked quietly. "You saw something. Whatever it was, it was so bad it made you sick. It's about that, isn't it?"

I didn't answer. She nodded.

"Yeah. It is. And you can't tell me?"

"I'm sorry," I said, but I didn't really mean it.

"I'm your friend, Amanda. That's why I'm here, getting involved in this insane mess. Because we're friends. If you're not telling me something—"

"I can't." I'd never told anyone. I couldn't start with Erin. I couldn't bear it. I'd already had so many of those side-eyed looks of pity just from people who even met my step-dad, heard how he talked to me — how could I tell a single person that he had a key to the bathroom, one of those slim little metal things you slid into the hole on the doorknob to disengage the lock? That I couldn't avoid that room but I was never safe in it — in fact, that it was the *least* safe place for me in the whole world? That all he had to do was catch me there when Mom wasn't home and for the next half hour I had to leave my body in order to stay sane?

That it was so horrible I'd somehow pushed it from my mind for the last fourteen years?

I couldn't. That was the simple answer.

Erin let out a long breath.

"Okay. Fine." She pursed her lips, then locked eyes with me. "I need to go home, I have to work early. Take your twenty-four hours to figure shit out without me. But if I haven't heard from you by—" Erin checked the screen of her phone. "—9pm tomorrow, I'm calling the cops. That's that. Okay?"

"Okay," I agreed. It was the best I could do; the DVDs had been coming pretty quickly so I figured it would be enough time. I hoped it would be... for Gretchen's sake.

"Okay," Erin said again, grabbing her purse and her shoes. She headed for the front door, then stopped and turned to me. "Why did you and Gretchen stop being friends?"

I told her the truth: "I can't remember."

Erin nodded slowly, mouth set in a grim line.

"That says a lot, Amanda," she said, and left.

I didn't sleep well that night. I spent most of it in broken, shuddery nightmares where I relived what happened in that bathroom over and over again. Sometimes I was a kid, sometimes I was older. In one particularly nasty one I was my 26-year-old self and god help me I actually liked it, the nightmare turned into some lurid guilty sex dream and I woke from that with a scream in my throat. I was drenched in sweat and had to run to the bathroom to vomit again.

I called in sick to work and sat backwards on my couch, staring out the window at the mailbox all morning.

No one came.

By noon I was really feeling the lack of sleep. My eyes were drifting closed; my head throbbed. Before I knew it I was jerking awake, startled and disoriented. I checked my phone: 2:32pm.

I only had until 9. I forced myself off the couch and went to check the mailbox and wouldn't you know it, the mail hadn't arrived yet but a slim clear plastic DVD case had. It read:

ACCIDENT 1999

My stomach lurched. Accident? What accident?

I brought it inside. Stuck it in my MacBook. I thought about calling Erin first then decided, *fuck it*, and clicked play.

The opening footage was of a car. Clay's car, the beaten-up teal Camaro he took so much pride in. I didn't recognize this video.

The camera zoomed in on the gas tank, which was open with the cap popped off. A hand was thrust in view, clutching a dirty rag. A small, pale, freckled hand.

Wait.

Wait.

Something was coming back to me.

"Gretchen?" I said, and at the same time the camera swung around to show 12-year-old Gretchen with her wire-frame glasses and a brightly-colored ski cap over her kinky red hair. She was grinning like she was proud of herself, pointing the camera at her own face.

"We're gonna get him back, Amanda," she said firmly. "We're gonna fuck up his car, ka-blooey, blow it to bits. He can't get away with what he did to you."

Wait...

"I'm doing this for you," Gretchen said, and suddenly there were tears in her eyes made so small by her thick lenses. "Because you're my best friend. That fucker deserves worse. I wish I could blow it up with him inside, but this will have to do."

Wait—

"I love you, Amanda," she said, and suddenly the footage cut away to the same dark bathroom from the other DVDs and my nightmares, but this time it was—

Oh god.

It was Erin.

She was wearing the same ski cap from the video. Her mouth was covered with duct tape and she was thrashing violently in a way Gretchen hadn't in the other DVDs.

I'd done this. I'd put her in danger, how could I have been so stupid? Of course whoever was behind this could see Erin coming and going, they'd been delivering the DVDs so why didn't I think about whether they were watching my house?

I watched her struggle for almost a minute before the video cut to black, and then —

REMEMBER NOW?

Then —

IF YOU'VE FIGURED IT OUT

And —

COME

I left my MacBook open, grabbed my keys, and ran to my car. The old house was twenty minutes away. I hoped I could get there in time.

———

BEST FRIENDS 2013

I ran three red lights on my way to the old house on Turner Street where I grew up. How I wasn't pulled over is some kind of miracle because I was easily doing fifteen over the speed limit but the important part is that I wasn't pulled over, I didn't pass a single cop the whole time. Good thing, too, because the very first DVD had laid out the rules — no cops.

The old neighborhood was just as I remembered it: small, dirty, and depressing as hell. Low-income housing seemed to have sank even lower in the ten years since I'd moved away.

My car screamed into the driveway of the little yellow tinderbox. There weren't any other cars parked outside; a sadly sagging FOR SALE sign was jammed into the badly-tended lawn, faded to almost white by the sun.

Now that I was here it occurred to me I'd have to actually go inside. My stomach lurched violently.

I was going to have to go into that house, into that bathroom where Clay stole my innocence over and over again. I was going to have to face whoever was sending the DVDs. My only comfort was that I knew it couldn't be Clay; he'd passed away in 2010. Brain aneurysm. Dropped dead in the middle of Home Depot while shopping for a new power drill.

I attended his funeral because he was my step-dad and Mom needed me there. She didn't know what he'd done and I couldn't remember, but the next day I went back to the graveyard alone. I stared at his grave for a very long time before gathering all the phlegm I had in my throat and spitting on the fresh dirt.

I hadn't known why I'd done that. Now I do.

I took a deep breath, steeled my nerves, and went inside.

The front door was unlocked; it was late afternoon but dreary-grey outside. No power, so the house was dark and every shadow felt ominous. I repressed the urge to call out "Hello?" like the dumb girl in a horror movie.

I crept quietly up to the bathroom and found I was wrong—there was power. A sliver of light shone from the crack at the bottom of the door. That made sense, Gretchen and Erin had been lit in each of the videos. It also meant she was in there.

I tried the doorknob. Locked.

Since when had the bathroom door being locked ever mattered?

I felt along the top of the doorframe for the slim metal key. Wouldn't you know it, there it was, just where Clay always left it. When I found his hiding spot I started throwing the key away but it didn't matter because they kept appearing, like he had a stash of them or something.

Fucker.

I slid the key into the hole in the metal doorknob and heard the familiar click of the lock disengaging. Slowly, carefully, I opened the door.

Behind a MacBook propped on some old plastic crates and a strategically-placed floodlight sat Erin. The ski-cap was gone but she was wearing Gretchen's old glasses, the wireframe ones; they made her eyes look like pinpricks. Erin has perfect vision so I knew she probably couldn't see a thing and I was right — she started thrashing violently against the chair, mistaking me for her captor.

"It's me, Erin, it's Amanda," I whispered, unsure where said captor was. I moved towards her and noticed that iMovie was pulled up on the screen of the MacBook. Must've been how they were making the DVDs.

Hearing my voice made Erin stop, then shake her head violently. She tried to speak but the duct tape kept her voice muffled. I couldn't understand a word she was saying.

Her wrists were tied behind her with that yellow plastic-y rope you buy when you tie stuff down in a moving van. The skin beneath it was rubbed raw, red and chafing.

"I'm gonna get you out of here," I said in a hushed voice.

But before I could look for something to cut through the rope I heard, "Well, aren't you a good friend."

I turned around and for a moment I couldn't see anything but a dark shape in the doorway; the floodlight was too bright. Then it went out and as my eyes adjusted I saw her.

Gretchen.

She was dressed normally now, just a plain pink t-shirt and jeans — no glasses or duct tape. Her bad eye sagged but beneath the destroyed scar tissue of her face, she was smiling, holding the unplugged cord of the floodlight.

"Gretchen?" I said, because I could think of nothing else to say.

"Oh, so you DO recognize me," she said, sticking out her lower lip. "I'm shocked. I mean, I've been sending these DVDs for a few days now but you never showed up so I was starting to suspect you didn't even remember who I was."

"Of course I recognize you," I said, stunned.

"Really? Because I think I put on a pretty good show but you didn't show up like Prince Fucking Charming to save ME." Gretchen gestured vaguely towards Erin with the end of the cord. "I had to up the ante and bring this one out here to get any sort of action out of you."

"I didn't know where you were." I stepped closer to her, wanting to put distance between Gretchen and Erin. Gretchen made a clucking noise with her tongue and produced a small black handgun from the back pocket of her jeans.

"Don't move," she said, pointing it at me. "Not another step."

Have you ever had a gun pointed at you? Your stomach goes all cold. It feels like the bottom has dropped out of your world and you're stuck in a freefall. But I didn't have time to be scared because it was Gretchen, Gretchen who'd been sending the DVDs and had never been in any danger at all and was clearly out of her god damn mind.

"I'm sorry I didn't come sooner," I said, trying to make my voice soothing, placating. "I didn't recognize the bathroom until yesterday and then you told me to wait for one more, remember?"

"You expect me to believe you?" she scoffed. "This bathroom was your fucking nightmare, Amanda, come on. Don't fuck around with me. I know you better than that."

"I'm telling you the truth." I kept my eyes on her face and tried not to look at the gun. "I repressed it, blocked it or something. I didn't even remember — remember what had happened here."

Her face softened a little but she didn't put the gun down.

"Do you remember what you did to me?" Gretchen asked quietly. "Do you remember this?" She touched the burn scars, the skin near the corner of her sagging eye.

"Not until you sent today's DVD," I said, and it was the truth.

Gretchen stayed overnight for New Year's Eve 1998. Clay and Mom had some stupid office party to go to so we were left home alone with popcorn and some movies from Blockbuster. He had the nerve to say he "trusted" us because we were such "big girls" now. Fucker even winked at me like the secret we shared was a tasty one.

That's probably the only reason I told her.

"If I tell you something, do you promise not to tell anyone else?" I asked hesitantly. We were watching *Balto*, one of my favorites, but I could hardly pay attention.

"You can tell me anything," Gretchen said, squinting at the screen. "You know, I think that goose is the fat detective from *Roger Rabbit*."

I paused the movie. She glanced at me, about to protest, then saw that I was chewing on my thumbnail. It was one of my tells when I was upset; that winter, I had chewed both of them down to the quick.

"What's wrong?"

I waited a moment, my throat working as I tried to get the words out, then suddenly I was crying, great heaving sobs bursting out of me like gunfire.

Gretchen put her arms around me and stroked my hair and soon enough I told her everything.

The next morning, I woke up much earlier than usual to find Gretchen missing. Clay and Mom were sleeping off the New Year's festivities so I snuck quietly around the house trying to see where she'd went. Her ski-cap was missing and so were her shoes.

Puzzled, I looked out the living room window to see if she was playing outside or something and there she was, standing next to Clay's Camaro. She was holding Clay's video camera, too, the big bulky one that recorded straight to VHS tapes. It was pointed at her face; she was saying something to it.

I slipped my parka over my nightgown and hurried outside. If she broke that thing I'd be in some serious shit.

"Gretchen, what are you doing?" I called from the steps. She glanced up, eyes wide behind her glasses.

"Oh dang, you weren't supposed to see this yet!" she complained. "It was gonna be a surprise!"

"What are you doing?" I repeated as I hurried across the cold pavement to meet her in the driveway. Gretchen turned the camera off and set it gingerly in the frosty grass.

"I'm blowing up Clay's car," she said, face beaming.

"You're — you're WHAT?" I looked at the rag in her hand and for the first time noticed the can of gasoline at her feet; it was the one Clay used to fuel up the lawn mower.

"With this," she said, waving the damp rag in my face. It reeked of gas. "I saw it in a movie. You soak some cloth in gasoline, stick it in the gas tank, light it, then — ka-blooey!"

"Gretchen, that's crazy," I said, shocked. I wasn't sure what I'd expected after telling her but not... this.

"He deserves it," Gretchen said firmly. "You told me what he's been doing to you, and we're just kids, no one will believe us over him. He'll win. This way, he loses SOMETHING."

She paused, thinking, then handed me the rag.

"You should do it. You should light it, you should be the one who does it."

"I don't want to do it," I insisted, trying to give the rag back, but Gretchen wouldn't take it.

"You have to. You'll feel better."

It was something about the way she said that, I still don't know what it was but I felt a vital part inside myself snap.

"Don't you get it, you dummy?" I cried, throwing the rag back at her. I threw it hard, harder than I should've, and it hit her in the face, covering one of her eyes. "I'm not going to feel better! I'm never going to feel better, I'm going to be broken for the rest of my life and nothing can change that and this is a *STUPID FUCKING IDEA!*"

Gretchen took the rag off her face and stared at me, hurt.

"I'm doing this for you," she said, sounding confused.

"I don't WANT you to do ANYTHING for me!" I screamed. It was coming out, all the anger and fear and self-loathing and it was directed at Gretchen which wasn't fair but it's what was happening. "We're only friends because I had to move to this shithole neighborhood and someday I'm going to go somewhere else and I'm *never going to think about you ever again!*"

She looked at me for a long time, like she was waiting for me to take it all back.

I didn't.

"Fine," Gretchen said at last, turning a light shade of pink beneath her freckles. "Fine." She looked down at the rag in her hand and seemed to make a decision. She fished one of Clay's cigarette lighters from her pocket and clicked it to life, intending to set the rag on fire. I guess she meant to throw it at me.

"Wait!" I cried, but it was too late.

The rag caught quickly but so did Gretchen. Her skin erupted in flames where I'd thrown the rag at her, most of the left side of her face. She began screaming. I've never heard a sound like that, before or after.

It didn't take long for her hair to go up, too, and she was just standing there, flailing, so I did the only thing I could do once my panic-stricken body decided to listen to me: I threw her down in the frosty grass of my front lawn, face first, and started slapping madly at her smoldering hair.

It just happened so fast. Mom heard us screaming and came running outside; after a brief moment of shock she reemerged with a wet towel which she threw over Gretchen, putting out the flames at once. Clay followed shortly after her and stomped out the burning rag where Gretchen had dropped it on the driveway. He looked at the rag, at Gretchen, at the open gas tank of his car. Looked at me. Then he went inside and called the police.

"You let them take me away," Gretchen said, now in the bathroom of my old house. She was still pointing the gun at me but had lowered it slightly. "I went to the hospital and then they sent me to a different hospital, a crazy person hospital, and you let them take me."

"I was just a kid," I said weakly.

"And what the fuck was I?" she demanded, raising the gun again. "I was a kid too, for god's sake, I was just trying to help you and you could've told them about Clay but you DIDN'T, Amanda, you just let them take me!"

I didn't say anything. What was there to say? She was right.

"And the worst part is," Gretchen said grimly, "that you visited me once. ONCE. In six fucking years."

"Clay wouldn't let me," I said in a small voice.

"Yeah right. You just didn't want to. Admit it. You said what you really thought that day in the driveway, say it now. You didn't want to see me because we weren't ever really friends."

"That's not true." My throat felt like it was closing up; tears stung hot in my eyes. "I didn't mean what I said, I was just upset and — and fucked up — of course you were my friend, Ducky, you were my best friend."

"Don't fucking call me that!" she screamed.

I winced but went on.

"I visited you the first week in the hospital because Clay was at work and I had bus fare but that was all I could do," I explained, trying not to cry. "He was watching me like a hawk, said I shouldn't hang out with the girl who tried to kill him and Mom backed him up and there was nothing I could do!"

Gretchen didn't say anything. She waited for me to go on.

"And then high school happened and I had to get a job to help out with the house and I just — I just got so — and then it got to where it was easier not to think about it, you know? Because he'd finally stopped, you scared him enough that I think he knew you knew and he STOPPED and eventually it was like it didn't happen and—" I drifted off, helpless.

"And when you moved out?" she asked, gun still pointed at me.

"I just wanted to get away from here," I said weakly. "I had to. I had to get away from this house."

"Like I said you would." Gretchen's mouth was a thin, grim line.

"I did come," I insisted. "I came to the hospital on my way out of town but you were so out of it, Gretchen, you wouldn't even look at me. You don't even remember. So I left, yeah, you're right. But it wasn't to get away from you. It was never that."

Gretchen let out a bark of humorless laughter.

"Seriously? You think I'm going to buy that bullshit? Please. You know what I think?" she said. "I think you didn't want to see me because you couldn't bear to look at what you did." She didn't gesture to her face but I knew that's what she meant, the destroyed flesh and drooping eye.

"I didn't get that gasoline out, Gretchen," I explained softly. "I'll take the blame for a lot of this but let's be fair: YOU did that. And you could've killed all of us, you know, that car could've taken out half the block."

"Now you sound like my fucking therapist," she said, and let out another humorless laugh. There was a pause; Gretchen looked at me, then Erin, then raised the gun higher, leveling it at my face. "How about I make us even? Wreck all that prettiness with a nice big hole through one of your cheeks?"

I froze, unwilling to say anything that might anger her more.

"Fourteen years, gone," she spat. "Fourteen. More than half of my life. And all I've got to show for any of it is this awful fucking face."

Gretchen cocked the gun. I felt my limbs go watery.

She paused, then looked past me at Erin. And then she did the worst thing yet: she smiled.

"You can have her," Gretchen said, then put the barrel in her mouth and pulled the trigger.

That was more than two years ago. Two years since Gretchen sprayed her blood and brains across the flower-and-vine wallpaper in the room where my step-dad used to rape me but I still see it in my nightmares. Sometimes they're both there, Clay and Gretchen, laughing at me. She holds the gun while Clay does what he does. It always ends the same way: she eats the bullet and I wake up screaming.

Erin and I don't speak anymore — well, no more than the polite "hey, how are you" on Facebook or an occasional "like" on one of our pictures. It's the 21st century way of ending a friendship, I guess.

I try not to think about it but my therapist says that's not right, it's what caused me to repress all these memories in the first place. I tried to explain to him the thing about avoiding sharp teeth but I'm supposed to work through it. So this is me, I suppose, working through it.

He also says it's not my fault. None of it — Clay, Gretchen, it wasn't my fault. I didn't ask to be raped. I didn't put the lighter in Gretchen's hand. Or the gun, for that matter.

I don't believe him.

They found a box of home movies in my old bedroom. VHS tapes. I think Mom must've left them behind when she and Clay moved out in 2007. Gretchen found them after being released from the mental hospital — I guess she just went straight to the house on Turner Street — and that's how the whole thing started. They've been sitting in my hall closet ever since.

For some reason, tonight, I've decided to watch them. All of them.

Who knows how many sharp teeth I'll find. How many times I'll get bitten by the barbs of my past. But it's something I have to do. Friendship bracelets and softball games and teen magazines and flowers being choked by weeds... I need to live it all again. It's the only way to leave my poisonous childhood behind.

The only thing I'm really afraid of — really, truly terrified of — is what else I'm going to remember.

5

WOMEN SEEKING MEN

The young man was what you'd consider conventionally attractive. He had dark, windswept hair and just the barest hint of stubble on his cheeks. He'd been skulking around the outside of her house for the better part of an hour.

Carissa was starting to get nervous. She had managed to ignore him for a while but there was no denying he was out there casing the place, just waiting for the sun to go down. There were only so many times someone could pass your place nonchalantly before it began to look not so nonchalant after all.

He was going to come inside, she just knew it. Would he break a window? Force his way in from the back porch? Or would he just try knocking on the front door, see if she'd be stupid enough to answer and then barrel through? Carissa was not a big girl, she was 5'4? and she ran to stay fit but she doubted she could stop him if he exerted any strength at all.

She peeked past the living room curtain again and found herself accidentally making eye contact with him as he strolled down the sidewalk, this time in the opposite direction from where he'd been going when she'd last spotted him, dark-furred hands deep in the pocket of his designer jeans. It reminded Carissa of those awkward moments in traffic when you glance to your right out of pure boredom and end up staring into the face of another driver who's decided to do the very same thing.

The young man averted his eyes as though he hadn't seen her and kept walking. She couldn't hear, but his lips were pursed as if he might be whistling.

Carissa picked up her phone from the coffee table. Maybe it was time to call her sister. Elaine would know what to do, would be able to coach her through it, that's what big sisters are for but for some stubborn reason Carissa didn't really want to, didn't want to admit defeat or that she needed help. As a woman who'd recently celebrated her 21st birthday, that sacred right of passage from girlhood to adulthood, she had this nagging sensation in her gut that said she needed to handle this herself.

The light outside was fading fast in that eerie way it does during late summer. You think the night will never come but suddenly the sky is melon-red and then blue-black in a matter of minutes, seconds it feels like, then the fireflies are winking in and out of existence and there it is, it's nightfall. Adulthood was sort of like that, too, Carissa supposed.

She chanced another peek through the curtains and was alarmed to realize the young man wasn't out there. He'd been keeping a tight track back and forth in front of the house, never really going much farther than he needed to, just barely out of sight until he could turn around and walk the same path again, but now he was nowhere to be seen.

That, and now it was dark. Or almost so. Dark enough, Carissa feared, that he was ready to strike.

Elaine could help, her worried mind insisted again. *Elaine would know just what to do, she's not that far, if you called her now she'd be here before he gets in.*

And then what? Spend the rest of her life calling Elaine every time shit got hard? "Save me, Elaine, help me, Elaine, you're always going to be the big sister and I'm always going to be the kid sister and I'll never be able to do anything on my own!"

Fuck that.

Carissa got to her feet and headed for the back door. She'd see if that had been left unlocked, she decided the front door was too obvious and he'd definitely try something more covert. First the back door, yes, then the door in the mudroom, then the garage door just for good measure—

Her scurrying thoughts came to an abrupt stop when she found herself being slammed against the wall, hard. Carissa's breath burst out of her in a surprised gasp; she hadn't even made it through the hallway to the kitchen and already he was inside.

Her hands scrambled to push him off her but he was fast, faster than she expected, and he gripped each of her wrists tight. With what seemed like very little effort, the young man forced her arms above her head and kept her pinned there like a butterfly in a glass display.

There was a brief moment where they locked eyes. Then he mashed his mouth against hers and she opened her lips to let him in.

The young man pressed his hips forward, grinding his erection slowly over the crotch of her jeans as they twisted their tongues together, pausing only to catch their breath. He tasted like whiskey and cigarettes, a combination that made her think, oddly, of her father's study.

He broke the kiss at last and they stared at each other, Carissa's arms still pinned above her head. Their chests heaved.

"Is this... is it okay?" he said finally in an unsure, halting voice. "Am I too rough or — I didn't know if I should try to scare you or not — like, am I doing it right?"

Carissa rolled her eyes, annoyed.

"What did the ad say?" she demanded.

He licked his lips nervously.

"'Must not be out-of-character during the experience,'" he recited like a small child delivering well-studied lines to a strict teacher. "I know, but like, I don't want to hurt you—"

Carissa shoved him off, taking him by surprise and breaking his grip easily.

"You know, when a girl posts on Craigslist that she wants a 'rape fantasy,' she's not looking for some pussy to ask her if they're doing it right." She leaned to her right to peer into the kitchen. "I mean, Jesus, you didn't even break a window or anything!"

"The door was unlocked," he said, sheepish.

"The entire *idea* is to be taken by force. By a *man*." Carissa rubbed her wrists which were, undeniably, a little sore. She sized him up — attractive, yes, in a dark sort of way, but clearly not a fighter. How disappointing.

"I'm sorry, I've never done this before." He ran a hand through his hair, then reached for her. "Want me to try again?"

Carissa batted him away.

"No, the moment is ruined! Just... give me a minute." She chewed on her thumbnail, considering her options, figuring out the best way it could go down. This was delicate work, after all.

Then she smiled. "Okay, I've got it. Follow my lead, okay?"

He grinned back at her, pleased to have another shot. He nodded vigorously.

"Yeah, oka—"

He was cut off by a sharp, stinging blow to his cheek. Dazed, he stumbled backwards, and Carissa took off down the hallway.

"Leave me alone!" she screamed, oddly pleased by how desperate she sounded. A regular Jamie Lee Curtis.

God, he really was dumb; it took him a few seconds to realize what she was doing. Then his lumbering footsteps came after her, heavy black boots pounding the hardwood floor.

Carissa rounded the corner, skidded on the carpet runner, then yanked open the door to the basement. She clambered down the stairs and left the door open for him, god forbid he couldn't figure it out himself.

If this was a horror movie, her character would've been one of those brainless bimbos who runs herself into a corner like a terrified mouse in a maze. There was an exit in the basement, sure, but the door was old and hard to open and you sort of ended up in this little stone stairwell where most of the steps had crumbled. Of course, she wasn't really looking for escape, but the scenario was amusing to say the least.

Carissa heard him stumbling down the stairs and pressed herself against the brick wall near the washer/dryer combo. It put her far from the door and gave her the best vantage point of him as he entered the basement.

As he approached her, looking much more like a predator than he had upstairs, she put on her best I'm-So-Very-Scared face.

"Please, don't," Carissa pleaded softly.

He took a few steps towards her, slow, menacing.

"You hit me," he growled.

"Please, no, no, I'm sorry!" He got closer, flexing his dark-furred hands into fists, baring his teeth. Dumb as he seemed, he really was pretty hot. What a shame.

He slammed those hands on either side of her head against the brick, actually catching her by surprise and making her cry out.

"Take. Off. Your. Pants," he said in a low voice, pressing the tented front of his jeans insistently forward. Well, well, well. Look who was finally participating.

"That's more like it," Carissa purred. She took him by the head and kissed him hard, threading her fingers through his thick hair. He kissed her back. He began fumbling at the button of her jeans.

Carissa withdrew, ran her tongue over her lips, and grinned.

"I don't think so," she murmured, then sank her teeth deep into the soft flesh of his throat.

He started to scream, but the scream turned into a sort of a strangled gurgle, liquid and sloppy. Carissa tightened her jaws, not giving him any leeway. He beat uselessly at the brick wall behind her.

The fingers in his hair dug their nails into his scalp. Blood began trickling down his cheeks, mingling with the blood pouring from his throat.

God, was it good. Even better than she'd expected. Rich and heady, like gourmet dark-brew coffee.

He was slowing down now, growing weaker. He kept slapping at the brick wall but they were silly little blows, halfhearted and feeble. Carissa noted with some amusement that he was still hard in his jeans; that too would fade once the blood flowed in another direction. And it would have to, wouldn't it, with that gaping hole in his neck!

When she was sure he had no strength left to run — not that it would matter, she doubted he could make it up the crumbling stone steps or out that door that stuck when you tried to open it — Carissa whipped her head back, bringing with it a large chunk of flesh and what she assumed was a bone fragment. Or maybe that was just muscle. Either way, it was gritty, and not as good as the rest of him.

He gaped at her, his mouth hanging open as he fell first to his knees, then face-forward onto the cement floor. She heard the crunch of his nose breaking and for some reason found it very funny.

Blood began to pool around his head in a syrupy puddle. Carissa wondered if she shouldn't have kept him upright, brought something with her to store it — like what, tupperware? A water bottle and a funnel? The idea of trying to pour him into an easily-preserved container also struck her as hilarious and she giggled hysterically.

Elaine would know what to do.

Wiping her mouth with the back of one hand, Carissa fished her phone out of her pocket with the other. She dialed her sister and considered whether the stains would come out of the top she was wearing. Probably not. Should've planned better for that, too. She looked hot in that top.

"What's up, Rissa?" Elaine chirped in her ear.

"I did it!" Carissa was surprised by how excited she sounded; she'd envisioned coming off all cool and collected but that idea went right out the window when her sister answered the phone. "I did it, my first time, I actually fucking *did it!* With no help or anything!"

Elaine squealed.

"Oh my god, Rissa, I'm so proud of you! Your first feeding, that's so awesome, have you told Mom and Dad yet?"

"No, not yet, I still have to—" She paused, nudging his lifeless body with her toe. "—clean up, I guess."

"Oh, so like you *just* did it? Wow, I can't believe it!" Elaine sounded like she was on the verge of tears. "My baby sister, twenty-one and feeding and all grown up!"

"Don't start crying," Carissa said playfully. "If you start crying, I'll start crying and I've got to take care of this guy!"

"Where'd you find him? A bar? House party?"

Carissa started laughing.

"No, I fucking *ordered* him on Craigslist like a pizza! I mean, I was a little scared, like I thought I couldn't do it unless I felt like he was going to hurt me or something, like if it was self defense I'd feel better — but I figured that part out myself."

"I knew you would. I'm seriously so, so proud of you. Tomorrow night, me and you, happy hour. My treat."

The blood pool was getting bigger. Carissa balanced the phone on her ear and scooted a laundry basket out of its reach.

"You bet. But first, um — can you help me? Tell me what to do with... the rest?"

"Of course," Elaine said warmly. "That's what big sisters are for."

6

DRAINS IN THE FLOOR

Back when I was in college, the student campus activity council hired a famous ghost hunter to come speak at our school. I've always loved the paranormal so I left my skeptical boyfriend behind in his dorm and hightailed it over to the auditorium.

The ghost hunter was someone I'd never heard of but he had an impressive background. He was a man of small stature with a little white professor's beard and a receding hairline, but the way he spoke about the afterlife was fascinating. You could tell he truly believed what he claimed to see — either that, or he was a hell of a salesman. He had us hanging on every word.

We watched some interesting video clips of his investigations. He had a nice collection of photos and scary stories to go with them; I remember one about a haunted doll that he said moved freely around the room of the person who had picked it up at a flea market, just not when anyone was around to witness it.

Towards the end he opened up the floor for questions. There were your typical dumbass college kid questions – "Have you ever seen someone's head spin around like 'The Exorcist'?", stupid stuff like that – and a few that were more serious, more polite. I decided I wasn't going to let this opportunity to speak to someone so apparently revered in the field of the supernatural slip away, so I raised my hand.

The ghost hunter spotted me, pointed, and smiled. "Yes, you, the girl in the white shirt?"

"Yeah, hi," I said, and I know I sounded nervous, because I felt so *dumb* for sounding so nervous. I mean, this guy was just a ghost hunter, not some rock star. "I was just wondering – what's the scariest thing you can remember from your career as a ghost hunter?"

I was halfway back in the auditorium, quite a distance from the stage, but I saw his face fall. I know I did.

"Well," he said, forcing a tight little laugh (it *was* forced, I *know* it was), "there are so many scary moments to recall; they tend to pop up quite often when you're in my line of work..."

This got a little chuckle from the audience. I suddenly felt pretty stupid for asking the question at all. My cheeks burned and I was glad he couldn't see me very well in the auditorium's low lighting.

He proceeded to tell some story about tracking a poltergeist in an abandoned elementary school and his flashlight failing. I remember because it really wasn't very scary; at least, it didn't seem that way for someone who hunts ghosts for a living.

He moved on and answered a few more questions. He seemed agitated. He didn't look my way again.

When it was over and everyone started to leave, I decided not to get stuck in the crush of students leaving through the front door. Feeling somewhat dejected, like I had done something wrong, I slipped quietly out the theater exit and headed for my dorm.

The ghost hunter was sitting outside on a bench near the bike racks, smoking a cigarette. I ducked my head and tried to get by without him noticing.

"Hey, kid." He took another drag and crushed the cigarette out on the cement bench beside him.

"Listen, I'm sorry," I remember blurting, feeling like such a stupid little girl, "I know my question was dumb, I wasn't trying to make fun of you or anything–"

He shook his head. He brushed the ashes off the bench. He patted the space beside him, inviting me to sit.

I hesitated–this could definitely be a case of stranger danger, just like they taught in the Intro to University classes–then sat down, keeping a healthy distance between us. He was old, I was young, I could probably outrun the guy. Or who knows, maybe I was just as stupid as I felt.

"I didn't tell the truth," the ghost hunter said. His face looked much older close-up, the wrinkles deeper. The confident salesman aura had faded from him, leaving behind a man in his sixties who had clearly seen a lot of things. A lot of frightening things. "That story I told, it wasn't the scariest moment of my career."

"I know," I remember saying. He nodded, as though he had known I knew.

"*This* is the scariest moment of my career," he said, and this is what he told me.

It was the 1970s; I was a much younger man, I hadn't reached success in the paranormal industry quite yet and was left to pick up the scraps that the pros didn't want. Usually the cases turned out to be schizophrenics whose broken minds tricked them into believing they were tormented by phantoms, or children playing pranks on gullible and concerned members of the neighborhood. If anything it was a simple cleansing of the home with sage and off I went. I spent much of those early years wishing I'd become a doctor like my mother had wanted.

When I first got the call I was ecstatic. What the client was describing appeared to be a full-blown demonic haunting, complete with physical manifestations, possession, and multiple witnesses. It was the break I was searching for. It was the break I *needed*.

The only detail that truly worried me was that their teenage son, the person they claimed to be suffering from possession, had become violent with members of his family. Up until recently he'd only acted out of character, moody; however, a week prior he had tried to rape his older female cousin.

She was shaken, but mostly unharmed. The family sent her to live with other relatives until it could all be figured out. Assuming, of course, that it *would* be figured out. People assume so much.

When I headed out to their home I made sure to arrive fully prepared. I brought holy water, crucifixes, sage, and–just for good measure–a small loaded handgun. I was quite sure it wouldn't come to that, but something about the mother's frantic tone over the phone told me it was just a good idea.

I wish I could say the visit itself was exciting. Unfortunately, from the moment I pulled into the driveway of the beautiful remodeled Victorian, all activity seemed to stop–that is, if it was ever there to begin with.

I spent two weeks investigating the home. I used equipment considered very technologically advanced for the era. I studied energy waves. I interviewed the son whose family claimed to be possessed when in fact he just seemed to be depressed, perhaps psychologically disturbed.

I recommended a therapist, a renowned child psychologist who was famous for his work with violent young men. On my last day in the house they took him into the city for treatment; his parents returned shortly before midnight, retiring wearily to their bedroom, leaving me alone in the kitchen to go over my findings.

Findings? What findings? There was nothing to be said, and I knew it. Everything they'd described could be written off to the hysterics of a family who couldn't admit their son was in desperate need of medical attention. Everything, that is, except for the drains in the floor.

Upon touring the home I was impressed with how up-to-date it had been brought; it was clearly from the early 1900s and kept in immaculate condition. The woodwork and character of the house was carefully preserved as it was given necessary updates, like modern plumbing and electricity. The basement was the only area that seemed stuck in time.

The walls were a clammy stone that was prone to gathering moisture, leaving it unfit to store anything vulnerable to spiders or mold. The family had left it empty for this reason and, while it certainly felt very spooky to spend any amount of time in the windowless room with the single hanging light and its vast cement floors, I never recorded anything of note in this area. Just a low sense of dread, but really, don't we all feel that in places where we expect to be afraid?

However, there was one thing I couldn't understand. Given the approximate time the home had been built and its presence in a residential neighborhood, there was simply no accounting for the four large slotted drains set in the cold concrete floor.

As I sat alone in the kitchen, poring over my meager findings, trying to find meaning in all these words, I heard something.

It was only a little noise at first and so I ignored it. But then it came again, louder this time. A scrape, or perhaps a sigh. The sound of fingers trailing along a wall.

There was a steep spiral staircase that led to the second floor, winding up from the corner of the small kitchen, and it was where the noise seemed to be coming from. Assuming it was simply one of the homeowners restless after dropping their son off in an institution, I glanced up.

It was coming down the stairs. I can't say walking, because that wasn't the case. It was just... floating isn't even the right word. Just *coming*. Coming down the stairs, straight at me.

It had no eyes. It had no *face*. And yet somehow I knew it was looking at me, right at me, into the very depths of my soul.

Then it spoke.

I'm not sure how it spoke—I don't think I actually *heard* anything, so perhaps it used some sort of telepathy? Either way I can recall the words to this very day:

"You know what he did to us."

I didn't think. I couldn't. I just ran.

I upended my chair when I fled, scattering papers across the kitchen that claimed this house wasn't really haunted, it was all the hallucinations of a very sick boy.

I left them there. Do you know how awful that is? I *left* those people in that house with that *thing*. I didn't stop driving for 30 miles, for god's sake. When I realized how far I'd gone I finally pulled over and called the family from a pay phone. They were the furthest thing from my mind when I saw it, all I could do was respond to the deep animal instinct to escape, to run out of that supposedly safe house with my tail between my legs.

I never went back. I couldn't. That *thing* might be there.

They moved, I think. I was unable to continue my investigation. In writing I cited insufficient evidence, but I knew it was cowardice.

I believe the house was leveled a few years later.

I ended up doing my own research. Curiosity ate away at me with vicious little rat teeth as time went by, the accusation still ringing fresh in my ears:

"You know what he did to us."

And eventually, yes, I did.

Old newspaper clippings didn't tie the stories together, not necessarily, but I was able to piece some meaning out of the yellowed excerpts. At some point around the turn of the century, the house had been residence to a well-respected mortician. Unable to find a building in town to suit his needs, he said, he built his own home/office space. It was a grand feat of architecture and a shining example of a true entrepreneur, a man pursuing the American dream of running his own business.

Upstairs, the bedroom. Mid-level, the funeral home. In the basement, a mortuary.

I knew what the drains were for.

Separately, decades later, another well-respected member of the local community was arrested under the suspicion of "abuse of his professional position" with "moral cause." The newspaper didn't elaborate, probably due to the sensitive nature of the crimes, but his punishment was minor;

after a brief stay in the local jail, the perpetrator stripped his home of all its value and left town before trial, never to be seen again.

It didn't take much to guess the connection. I suppose I don't know for sure, but the words of that thing still echo through my head to this day:

"You know what he did to us."

There was a reason that mortician felt such a strong desire to build a house that contained his business, to "suit his needs."

The things that were done to those bodies in the basement were unspeakable. But yes, I know. I know what he did to them.

And it's because of this, coming face to face with the true nature of man in its darkest places, that the encounter with that featureless thing is the scariest moment of my career.

Because now I know.

———

I still remember his expression, the way all the color dropped out of him as he went on, the white hair of his beard barely distinguishable from his pale skin. The slump of his shoulders. The way his voice shook.

I apologized. He waved me off. He left.

I felt terrible, I *still* feel terrible for making him relive that moment. But, as I grew up, as campus activities were replaced with bills and my own career, the ghost hunter fell from the forefront of my mind little by little.

Until last week, when I moved in with my fiancé. When I took the boxes into the basement despite his warnings of spiders and mold.

Because there's a large slotted drain in the center of the room.

And I'm so worried, so scared, about what I might know.

7

I HOPE MY SISTER DIES SOON

It's not easy having a twin. Someone who looks like you, thinks like you. Someone who can get inside your head, sticky little fingers poking around even though you ask her nicely to stop.

Jean and I are identical but there's something different about Jean. You know it right away. Jean is quiet. She doesn't like to talk to other people. She only talks to me—talks with her eyes, with her mind. I want to talk to other people but Jean won't let me.

Jean wants me to be just like her. Or Jean wants to be just like me. Does it matter? How *can* it matter when we look exactly the same, the mirror image of a girl, essentially the same effect as if your vision had doubled and one wasn't even there at all?

When we were younger everyone thought it was cute, how alike we looked. Mommy and Daddy smiled at us in our matching dresses, holding hands like tiny porcelain dolls, sweet and inseparable. But it's only cute when you're little. Get a bit older, keep wearing the matching dresses and holding hands, well — people can't help but think of those girls from *The Shining*.

Jean likes the matching dresses. I don't.

But what I like doesn't matter because Jean always gets her way. When she doesn't, or even *thinks* she might not, Jean throws tantrums. Not the normal kind of tantrums where you kick and cry and demand whatever thing it is you desire. Jean's tantrums are worse.

They tried to make us normal, thought that maybe separating us in school would be a good idea. I could tell from the screams ripping through my skull that it wasn't, but it still took the first week of third grade for the counselors to retrieve us from our different classrooms and send us home to Mommy.

Jean had just...stopped. Stopped everything—eating, drinking, almost blinking—in a form of catatonic protest. She wanted me to do the same. She called out to me from across the school, telling me it was what needed to be done. I covered my ears. I didn't want to hear her, but how can you silence something that's in your head?

I liked my new class. I wanted to make new friends. I tried to keep this hidden from her, cradled it in my mind like something made of delicate glass, but I should've known by then there was no keeping a secret from my sister.

Jean had been furious when the teacher led her down the hall away from me but that was *nothing* compared to when she looked inside and saw my blossoming hope to become my own person, someone Jean couldn't touch. In my head she screamed and cried and threw tantrums and gripped my throat with her sticky invisible fingers until I gave in and stopped eating too.

It's like being in an echo chamber with your own voice shrieking at you. You know it's *not* you and yet, somehow, it is.

Mean, vicious little fingers, always digging and poking where they didn't belong. In a place that should've been my own but never had been. Always there, ready at a moment's notice to seize my tongue should I try to speak against her. I grew up learning not to fight. Jean's the stronger twin, she always has been from the moment we slipped out of Mommy, two infants in perfect replica – one screaming, one silent.

You're supposed to love your sister. Aren't you? When I search my heart for that feeling I always come up empty, and yet there's still that phantom cord running between the two of us, a kind of passageway from my mind to hers like the tunnels that ran under ancient asylums.

It hurts to see other girls together, laughing and having fun, talking with more than just the murmur of their minds. The sound reminds me of dry cornstalks in autumn, whispery and somehow ominous.

When we were thirteen, we began to bleed on the same day, at the same time. I was excited but Jean hated it, hated the thick liquid coming out of us like dark red afterbirth, refused to even acknowledge the fact that we'd become women and so we sat together on the couch in dead silence, Jean stewing in her impotent rage against something she couldn't control.

I tried to explain. I took her hand gently in mine. I spoke to Jean's mind of the moon and the tides and what we'd learned about our changing, shifting bodies. She responded by digging her fingernails into my palm, bringing forth a new flow of fresh blood.

Sometimes I stared at the stains left behind on the cushion and tried to find meaning in them like a dried-blood inkblot test. It struck me to see how different they were, their seeping edges not identical in the least, and yet if you looked for long enough, they seemed to be the same after all.

Mommy tried to scrub them out but they remained, twin ghostly brown splotches marring her beautiful white couch. In the end, she threw a slipcover over it and that was that.

Mommy tried. That's what's important. She tried a lot of things to get Jean to be normal – to get *us* to be normal, together – but just like the couch it was simply a lost cause. Jean would sit there and stare at Mommy, her eyes like cold little flakes of metal, and ignore whatever had been presented to her: toys, games, demands, tears. It hurt to see Mommy so sad but my tongue was a useless slab of meat in my mouth. I couldn't tell her it was okay, that I loved her, that I hated how Jean's face was hard and mean and so similar to my own I felt like I was the one making her cry.

Last week, I heard her crying in her bedroom. She does it a lot these days.

I stood outside her door and caught the low murmur of Daddy's soothing words, trying to calm her down, but the weak sound of her weeping didn't change. She was so upset, whispering between sobs to Daddy about "facilities" and "better places." Somewhere to send us away.

I knew what this meant. Other children, normal children, they talk to their parents. They laugh and smile and hug. They don't hold hands and stare and talk only with their minds, only to each other. They point and laugh at children like us.

I mean, it makes sense. Mommy tried.

Daddy held her and said that maybe it was for the best. After all, we didn't seem happy. Maybe in some new place we'd come out of our shells, as though the whole thing was something we'd someday outgrow. I opened my mouth to tell them it was Jean, it's always been Jean, it's been Jean for seventeen years but my tongue was a heavy stone.

He told her they should try to break it to us over milk and cookies. Make it easier.

I buried this new knowledge in my head but Jean found it, she always does, digging away with her grubby little fingers in the soft parts of my mind. I suppose I shouldn't have been surprised when she met me in the hallway outside Mommy and Daddy's bedroom, those hard eyes glinting at me. I tried to make my mind like a still pond on a windless day.

But it was too late. Jean always gets what she wants.

She took my hand in hers and led me to the kitchen. She got the jug of milk out of the fridge and set it neat as you please on the counter. She looked at me and demanded, silently, that I fetch the rat poison from beneath the sink.

I tried frantically to dive my own unpracticed fingers into Jean's mind to see what she had planned; Jean pushed them away with no effort at all and instead produced a single clear image for me: the four of us on the dining room floor, dead and twisted, the poisoned milk spilled around us. It soaked into Mommy's hair and Daddy's shirt but it didn't matter because Jean had gotten what she wanted – she'd rather be dead on her own terms than locked away, and she'd rather take us with her.

I've always known there was something different about Jean but, for all her cruelty, I never expected this.

Or did I? Is it just easier to believe her incapable of murder because she's a monster that has my face?

She gave me a little mental push, annoyed at me for keeping her waiting.

Get the rat poison from beneath the sink.

Her tone was so flat, so matter of fact, that for a moment I wished I could kill her myself. Take my fingers – my *real* ones – and wrap them around her throat. Squeeze until the light went out of those cold eyes. End this madness once and for all. But I couldn't. I told you, I'm not like Jean.

So instead, I pushed back. I told Jean no.

Jean stared at me, unflinching, and pushed again.

Get the rat poison from beneath the sink.

No, Jean.

Get it.

We stared each other down, one girl as a mirror image standing silently in the kitchen's sunny afternoon light.

She didn't move but I felt her invisible grip tighten around my throat, shutting off my flow of air, bullying me once again into doing what she wanted, always what she wanted!

NO, JEAN!

And I found suddenly, miraculously, that I could do it too.

My phantom fingers closed around her neck and I saw her eyes go wide, eyes that could've been my eyes, eyes that were never scared unless I caught a glance of my own reflection but it wasn't now — Jean was scared.

She let go of me then. She stared, unblinking, unbelieving. Her mind, for once, was silent.

She took the milk and put it away, an expression less of defeat and more of someone who's decided they didn't want milk after all.

I don't know where she went, but Jean stayed quiet for a long time. I felt her fingers probing at me, gentle now that they knew what I was capable of, but I began shooing them away like flies off warm food.

Yesterday, she came to me in our bedroom and sat on her bed. She waited a moment, as though she understood the gravity of the situation very well indeed. As though I could end all this silliness now, if only I backed down.

But I didn't. I met her gaze, the eyes that could've been mine if they weren't so cold, and drilled one hard thought straight into her brain.

I hate you.

So Jean struck me a deal.

We could either exist fully together, or fully apart. There was no room for middle ground. We were one, or there would only be one left.

I can't be silent for my whole life. I want to cry out to my parents that I'm normal, I'm all right, I don't need to go away and I love them very much, even though Jean's never let me say so. Even though they think I'm like her.

She'd never believe it, but the only thing Jean and I share is a face. Nothing more.

And so here we are, twin girls in twin hospital beds, our fevers rising, organs shutting down. The doctors are baffled. They're running test after test but no one knows what's wrong... except us.

I've managed to keep her out of my head so far, but I'm getting weaker. I can feel her struggling for the upper hand. She's *furious*. I can feel rage wafting off of her like heat off a forest fire. She's always been the stronger twin, and she's never lost before.

I'm going to see if I can stop her kidneys now.

I hope my sister dies soon.

8

DOVERE

_____

He was sleeping so soundly it nearly changed her mind. At the very least, it gave her pause. She'd been quite sure of herself before entering the bedroom, dead set on doing what needed to be done, but now the sight of him curled on his side tested her resolve. The room was silent aside from his measured, even breaths and the ticking of the decorative clock on the wall.

He hadn't heard her come in. She wondered briefly if he'd taken sleeping pills. It was a new habit, a coping mechanism she supposed; it often left him groggy and sluggish.

She knew what she had to do, but it was hard when he looked like a little boy lying there, his mouth open just slightly. He looked like he had when they were young.

It was hard and she never imagined it would come to this but it was what had to be done. There was no other choice.

She placed the barrel of the gun to his head, square on the right temple where she had read a shot had the most potential for a fatality. In her research she had discovered 10% of people who take a bullet to the brain survive. It was a statistic that alarmed her but all she could do was try.

He must not have taken sleeping pills after all because at the touch of cold metal on his skin he opened his eyes. He tried to turn, opened his mouth to say something, but she forced his head back to the pillow with the barrel and pulled the trigger.

She was prepared for the noise but not for the blood. She waited a moment to be sure he wasn't moving before calmly setting the gun down on the nightstand and heading to the bathroom. She rinsed her arms and face in the sink. The water ran pink down the drain.

When she was as clean as she was going to get, she returned to the bedroom door and closed it.

It was what had to be done, she knew that, but it didn't make it any easier. She'd loved him, after all.

She walked through the living room, past the kitchen, out the screen door to the backyard. He hadn't put the hammock away the last time he'd been outside so she went barefoot through the grass and settled herself into it. It took some doing but soon she was comfortable.

She'd wished there was another way but there was only one bullet and besides, she wasn't sure she could put the barrel to her own temple and pull the trigger anyway.

Above her, the meteor that had been on the news for months hovered in the pale sky like a sinister black balloon.

He had insisted things would work out, that the scientists would find a way to redirect it or destroy it or whatever, an endless list of foolish optimisms that she knew were only for her benefit. He was as scared as she was, as scared as they all were, but he was the man and he had to save face. In her experience it was the women who made the tough calls when it came down to the wire and, if the latest reports were to be believed, this was the wire.

She would not see him die in flames and terror. She would not watch the man she loved, the man who'd held such strong resolve since they'd first heard about the impending apocalypse, reduced to a weeping child in the face of his own doom. She knew what had to be done and she'd done it.

The sun disappeared behind the meteor, which was enormous and getting bigger by the moment. Getting closer.

She closed her eyes as the darkness descended and thought about how he looked when he was sleeping.

9

CLOSE THE DOOR AND HAVE A SEAT

Studies show that Friday is the best day of the week to fire someone. Sorry, "let someone go." That's the politically-correct, touchy-feely-bullshit term, right? I guess it lets them down easier when they wake up with nowhere to be on a Saturday rather than a Tuesday.

Terminating employees isn't a job most people want because it's dirty work, something that makes your Average Joe feel slimy and mean. But not me. Guys like me know sometimes you have to be mean to survive. I'm damn good at it, too, though I suppose it's not something you'll ever hear me bragging about in a bar.

So good, in fact, they called me "The Axe." As in, "getting the axe." Cheesy, but most people are.

That's something you learn in my line of work. Most people fall into neat little categories. It's just something that happens when the line into your office is just as long as the one coming in the front door. People are cheesy, pretentious, useless. We like to think we're special, but ultimately, we're all the same. No one is an original. Not anymore.

Anyway. The nickname, cheesy as it may be, was both feared and respected. A call to my office was basically a death knell; countless men and women left in tears to find a box on their desk waiting to be filled with whatever meaningless crap they'd accumulated in their time with the company. I don't know where the boxes came from. That wasn't part of my job.

That Friday, I got word there was an axe to drop. An older guy, Steve Woodruff. No one I knew off the top of my head. A quick glance at his file proved this fact amusing; he'd been with the company for almost 20 years. Salesman.

Do you really want to know what he sold? No? Of course not. He's someone you'd brush off if he called you on the phone, a guy standing on your porch that you peer at behind the curtains and hope like hell that he'll leave. You don't care about him either. Be honest with yourself.

His productivity had fallen over time, slowly at first, then drastically in the past few months. He was barely making any sales. When he left for cold calls, there were doubts he was actually on the road, but perhaps holed up somewhere else. Drinking, maybe. Rumors in an office can get nasty. He was costing us money, that's the bottom line. Time to cut and run.

No severance package. No pension.

No skin off my ass.

I wish I could tell you I remembered it. I really do. But that afternoon I had a doctor's appointment and a lunch date with the guys in marketing and there may have been one too many martinis yet in the end the reason I don't remember is because there had been so many like him before. I'm sure he probably cried, or went pale and silent, or called me the devil. Those were the top three typical reactions to The Axe doing what he does best.

I hate that nickname. I really do.

So Steve came into my office and left my office, regardless of my inability to remember it. I'm sure he found the box on his desk. Security escorted him out.

Two hours later, Steve came back.

The same security guard that walked him to his car got it first. The point-blank shotgun blast blew most of his head off, splattering his brains across the hot-rod calendar behind his desk in the front lobby.

It's a fairly small office building so I'm sure some people heard it but the first inclination humans have when they hear something so unexpected, so out of the ordinary, is to assume it's something not out of the ordinary at all. Without the security guard to hit the silent alarm Steve walked right through the foyer and into the receptionist's office. Cheryl saw the gun, I think, and began to scream. She only got one wavering note out before the crack-boom of the bullets firing into her stomach cut her off.

Steve moved from her office to the advertising department. Here, he took out two of the guys in marketing, then paused to reload the shotgun. The copywriter got brave and tried to bolt but Steve was between him and the door and apparently more quick-fingered than he looked because the shells were in the gun and he fired one dead-eye shot into his back, sending him flying across the hall.

By this point the sound of the shotgun was too real to be ignored and people started to panic. The remaining employees, a motley mixture of HR and sales, bolted for the fire escape only to find it locked. Steve had, prior to his arrival in the lobby, chained the doors from the outside. They struggled against the crush of their own animal hysteria, unwilling to believe the door wouldn't open.

He picked these people off easily. Boom, boom, boom. They were screaming but then they weren't screaming anymore. I could hear it from under my desk. Somehow the silence was so much worse than the screaming.

Boom. Boom.

In my haste to protect myself I had completely forgotten to dial the police, but when I ducked my head out I heard Steve coming back my way, the metallic clicking sounds of the shells being exited from the gun and the new ones reloaded, the slow methodical plodding of his shoes on the thin office carpet. The Axe may be called many things, but that day I learned "brave" is not one of them. I dropped back under the desk and huddled there, trying to ignore the warm seep of my bladder letting go.

He entered my office and stood there. All I could hear was the strangely even sound of his breathing and the war-drum beat of my heart pounding in my ears.

"Remember me, boss?" Steve said softly, and for one wild moment I actually didn't, I couldn't even recall my own name if you'd asked me I was so terrified.

"You don't have to do this, Steve," I croaked, my mouth suddenly as dry as if you'd packed me full of hot desert sand. "There's still time, you can turn yourself in—"

"There's no time, you smug idiot." His voice was so calm, so pleasant, it was somehow far worse than if he'd been shrieking at me, because instead it was like we were chatting about the weather or the latest baseball game and ignoring the fact that the rest of the office were laying in cooling puddles of their own blood. "The police are on their way. Or they will be. Did you call them, boss?"

"Steve, please—"

"No. You had your chance to talk. Now it's mine." There was a quiet rolling sound as he pulled one of the office chairs up to the front of my desk, just as he had done two hours ago when I asked him to close the door and have a seat.

A long, terrible moment passed. The smell of my own urine was sharp in my nostrils.

"I begged you not to fire me. Do you remember that? You smelled like booze, so maybe you don't." Steve took in a deep breath, as though he could still smell the lunchtime martinis wafting off my skin. "'Productivity.' That was it, wasn't it? Why I got the axe? My 'productivity' had decreased?"

When I didn't answer, Steve banged the top of my desk with the butt of his shotgun.

"Yes!" I blurted.

"Hard to be productive, boss, when your wife is dying. When the cancer has eaten so far through her brain that she doesn't even know who you are even though you're at her bedside every day. When she's only able to speak in soft little screams because the pain's so bad."

He paused.

"What was the rumor?"

"What?" The word fell off my tongue like a heavy stone.

"The rumor. About me. Where I was when I wasn't on sales calls." I didn't know what to say, I groped through my memory like a blind man in the gutter but found nothing. This time Steve kicked the front of the desk; the sound was uncomfortably close. "Drinking?"

"Drinking!" I agreed in a yelp.

Steve sighed.

"That's rich, coming from you. No, I wasn't drinking. Visiting hours at the hospital are hard to accommodate with my schedule." There was another pause, and when he spoke again, I could somehow picture him smiling. "Do you have any idea how expensive cancer medicine is, boss?"

"No," I said at once.

"No," Steve echoed, sounding almost amused, "of course you don't. I bet you know how much a country club membership costs. Or a Porsche. Or those smug fucking Dior suits you wear. Do you even notice the rest of us walking around in our secondhand clothes?" Before I could respond he banged the desk again. The noise above my head was like a crack of dynamite and I felt my whole body jerk as if I'd been shocked.

"No," he said again. "Of course you don't."

He breathed in deeply through his nose.

"You ruin people's lives," Steve murmured. "What people work at for years, their *livelihoods*, the thing that keeps them getting up in the morning... you wipe it away with a few words and a box on their desk. And I bet you sleep like a goddamn baby."

"I'm sorry," I whispered, and I wish I could tell you that was true, that I truly felt the error of my ways and had learned a lesson. I really do.

"No you're not." There was a brief rolling sound as he stood up from the chair. "But you will be."

The shotgun clicked as he cocked it. My life began to flash before my eyes, my whole stupid materialistic life, the cheap women and expensive cars, every useless meaningless second and oh god if only I could have more of it...

Boom. Thump.

Silence.

And then it was just me, alone in the office of the dead. The only survivor of a madman's massacre. The lucky one.

Do you know what it's like to listen to the stillness of a place that was once full of life? To hear nothing but your own terrified heartbeat deep in your skull and what must be the sound of blood and brains pooling on the carpet?

It's deafening.

At some point, when the soaked front of my pants began to grow cold and stiff, I got out from under my desk and dialed 911.

There were ambulances. Someone put a blanket around my shoulders. I watched as they carried out body after body after body.

They were dead. All dead. But I was alive. I'd been spared. Why? Does the why even matter? Aren't we all beyond why at this point?

I went home and fell right to sleep. What else was there to do? You'd think I'd be wide awake but no, oh no, The Axe went home after the mass murder of his entire office building, changed his pants, had a beer, and went to sleep like a goddamn baby.

It was only then that I understood.

Every time I try to sleep, every time I close my eyes for more than a moment, when I drift off to that place of not-quite-conscious and not-quite-unconscious, I'm back at work.

I'm outside my own office. My suit is cheap and threadbare, my shoes don't fit quite right. I reach for the door and push it open.

Behind my desk sits Steve. The back of his head is a bloody mess, one giant exit wound from where he put the shotgun in his mouth, the mouth that smiles at me as he gestures a Dior suit-clad arm towards the chair in front of him.

He tells me to close the door and have a seat.

And every night, every fucking night for the past five years, I wake up screaming.

10

THE SKINSTEALER

I never meant for it to happen.

I know what little good that does now but I have to say that every day otherwise I'll totally lose it. If I don't remind myself that it was an accident, the careless actions of a little boy who had no idea the hurt he could do, that last shred of sanity will slip away like a scrap of paper caught in the wind.

It was 1993. I had recently turned eleven, that age where boys start to get hair in strange places and become incredibly mean to somehow compensate for it. I hadn't gotten it quite yet – the hair nor the meanness – but I could sense it spreading through my classmates like some exotic virus. A few of them shot up a few inches in height, towering over me in gym class; Jeff Porter was sporting what he called a mustache but was really just a few weird kinky sprouts above his lip.

I waited for my own transformation with barely concealed impatience. The only comfort seemed to be that my best friend Kevin was in the same boat, bobbing sadly behind our peers on the treacherous sea of puberty. He used to joke that at least we didn't smell as bad as the others, and *that* was true – they all seemed to reek like skunks, as though growing up caused you to develop stink glands along with underarm hair.

I liked Kevin. He could always make me laugh.

I *liked* him. I never meant for it to happen.

It was late October, a few days before Halloween, when I invited him to my house for one of our weekly sleepovers. We'd been having them since we were little kids and they seemed as natural to me as dinner at 6 o'clock every evening.

"Tomorrow's Friday," I told him as the school bus lurched its way towards our stop. "Sleepover at my place?"

Kevin was shouldering his bag when I first saw it, the flicker of unease that passed over his features. For some reason Jeff Porter snickered in the seat behind ours.

"Yeah man. Maybe. I dunno." Kevin got to his feet before the bus braked, almost sending him hurtling towards the front.

"Yeah, or I dunno?" I looked from Jeff Porter, that shitty mustache like pubes above his lip, and Kevin. Trying to figure out the joke I'd missed. The door of the bus opened with a metallic shriek and Kevin was already down the stairs, around the corner, heading down the street towards our houses. "Hey, wait up!" I called, hurrying after him.

Kevin slowed a little and allowed me to catch up. He watched with wary eyes as the school bus pulled away.

"What's your problem?" I demanded when I reached him, winded.

He took a moment to choose his words as we walked.

"The sleepovers, Jason. I mean... we're kinda old for those now, right? Don't you think?"

I was confused. We were eleven, we weren't too old for anything yet. In fact, I often felt too young – the things I wanted most were usually met with that exact response: R-rated movies, a later bedtime, a sip of dad's beer.

"No," I answered flatly, then backpedaled when I saw the distress on his face. "Well, I mean, do you think so?"

Kevin kicked a rock without enthusiasm.

"Maybe. It's just, I dunno, a baby sort of thing. We did it when we were kids, we're in middle school now." He shrugged a little, then looked back up at me. "Jeff Porter has a mustache."

"Jeff Porter eats shit," I spat, angrier than I meant to be, but it made Kevin laugh so that was good. I was still trying to figure out what was happening here.

"Sure, you're right about that," he said, grinning. "I just mean things are changing, you know? Things are gonna be different and we gotta be ready. If the other guys find out we're still having sleepovers, they're gonna say–" Kevin stopped abruptly. That look was back on his face. I didn't like it.

"They're gonna say what?" I stopped walking. After a few steps, Kevin stopped too and turned back to me.

"Never mind." He sighed deeply, then put a hand on my shoulder. I didn't like that either, like he was so much older and wiser than me. My birthday was a month before his, for god's sake. "One last one? One last sleepover, tomorrow night, we'll do it right with popcorn and movies and shit. Like old times."

"Okay," I said, even though I wasn't aware the old times had passed. I thought old times wouldn't be a real thing because Kevin was my best friend and isn't the saying best friends forever? Isn't that what the bracelets say?

Bullshit. Only girls get those dumb things, I guess.

"Okay," Kevin agreed, and then we walked the rest of the way home like everything was fine. Like old times.

Friday night came and so did Kevin. He brought his faded old red duffel bag, just like always. My mom made pizza rolls for dinner–she was unaware that this was THE LAST SLEEPOVER, as I'd come to think of it in important capital letters, but she was a great mom and she also rented a VHS copy of *The Mighty Ducks* for us. We made popcorn. We watched *The Mighty Ducks*. We laughed.

You'd think I'd remember the good parts the most clearly, right? That those cherished memories would've been etched in my mind forever so I could, at least, relive those last moments of my childhood when I most needed them.

Nope. Not fair, but still, nope.

The night had reached that wonderful time when parents went to bed and the sleepover went on, the door to my bedroom closed and our voices lowered. We could stay up for hours this way and often did. It made me sad to know this was the last time, that from now on I'd be staying up late without anyone else for company on Friday nights, no one to read comics with by flashlight or ask, "Are you still awake?" long after we should've been.

I wanted it to go on forever. I didn't want to go to sleep and have it be done with. THE LAST SLEEPOVER.

I came up with the idea while Kevin was in the bathroom. We could tell scary stories. That always got us wired up, too scared to go to sleep but too brave to admit it. It would get me a few extra hours with Kevin, at least. And that's all I really wanted.

"Okay, scary stories," I said when he came back into the bedroom, situating himself inside the sleeping bag beside mine. It read 'KEVIN' in big bold Sharpie letters near the part where it unzipped because his mother was convinced someone would steal it when he went to sleepaway camp three years ago. I knew that because we were friends and friends told each other everything, like how their mothers ruined their sleeping bag.

"Jason." He said it in that same infuriating tone that he had used when we were walking home. Like he knew so much more than me.

"We haven't told any in a long time," I protested. "Listen, I've got some really good ones, I'll go first–"

"Jason–" Looking at the clock.

"There was this couple who went to park at Lookout Point to make out–"

Now he gave me a smug glance.

"Hook on the handle."

I thought for a minute.

"So this girl is at a party and they dare her to go to the graveyard–"

"She put the knife through her skirt and thought it was a ghost and died of fright."

"Dammit, Kevin," I said, frustrated. Kevin laughed.

"That one's stupid anyway. Who dies of being scared? Not even possible."

"Okay, shut up, I know I've got a good one. Let me think." I was losing him and I knew it. I rifled through my mental files and folders, trying to come up with the right thing that would keep his attention, that would keep him awake.

"I've heard all your stories," Kevin said, turning over in his sleeping bag.

And then I had it. A new story, one I'd heard over the summer when he was at sleepaway camp with his ruined sleeping bag and I was at Boy Scout camp. Kevin wasn't a Boy Scout so he wouldn't have heard it. I was sure that would get him.

"Bet you've never heard of the Skinstealer," I said slyly. Kevin, who'd turned his back on me, was quiet for a moment.

"Go on."

I straightened a little and cleared my throat, assuming the role of the storyteller. This one couldn't be rushed. I had to tell it *good*.

"Okay. Legend has it that there was this undertaker, a really weird dude."

"Most undertakers are weird," Kevin muttered, his back still to me.

"But this guy was *extra* weird. Real skinny, real tall. He lived in the basement of the funeral home where he worked and he *never* left. For a long time people left him alone and didn't bother him unless, you know, someone they knew died. Then they used his services. And he was pretty good at it. Even though he was weird, people said he could make their dead family members look almost like they were ready to get up out of their caskets and walk away."

I paused for dramatic effect. Kevin didn't say anything. He didn't move. I went on.

"What they didn't know was that he was sick. He had some sort of blood disease, or maybe cancer. Whatever it was was eating him away. He was getting skinnier, looking worse all the time. And then came the car accident. That's what started it, they think."

Kevin rolled over in his sleeping bag and stared at me. It felt good to have his attention. I went on like I hadn't noticed.

"Someone brought in their daughter who'd been killed in a car wreck. The undertaker worked on her for days and finally told the family that she was too mangled in the accident to fix properly. He suggested a closed casket funeral, and the family agreed." I paused again.

"And?" he asked.

"And," I said, "suddenly, *every* funeral was a closed casket. Every body that was brought to him, he said he'd 'done his best' but they just weren't fit for viewing. Some people thought it was because he was getting sicker, that he had lost his touch. They were partly right."

"Finally, one family brought him a woman who had died pretty young in childbirth. They said she was beautiful in life and she was beautiful even when she had died and they wanted to see her. He tried to stop them from opening the casket but it was too late."

"What was inside?" Kevin asked. His eyes were wide.

"Nothing but bones," I said, and his eyes widened a little more. "Bones and stones to weight the casket down. See, he'd been taking each dead body and stripping the skin from it. He still did his undertaker duties by disposing of the organs and the blood, but all he left was the bones." I licked my lips, then added, "They found the skin he'd stolen from all the bodies. It was in the basement. He'd sewn all the pieces into a big blanket with thick black thread connecting each patch, like a quilt."

"Shit," said Kevin.

"Shit is right," I agreed.

"Why'd he do it?"

"That's the thing. When they asked him why, he said, 'I'm so cold, and it keeps me warm at night.' And then, he said, 'They weren't using it anyway.'"

"Jeez." Kevin seemed to consider this, then sat up in his sleeping bag. "So what happened to him?"

"People say he just disappeared, but some think that members of the town got together and took care of him on their own. You know, as revenge for what he did to their loved ones. They swore each other to secrecy and to this day, the Skinstealer walks the night, looking for more skin for his blanket. He's still... so... COLD!"

When I shouted 'cold' I grabbed Kevin by the shoulders, executing the classic jump scare at the end of our ghost stories. You didn't do it every time, see, because they'd sense it coming. But if the story was good enough, and you did it just right, it could be both terrifying and hilarious.

Kevin jerked out of my hands, a look of disgust on his face.

"Don't!" he spat.

I felt like I'd been slapped. Maybe he thought about it. He looked like he wanted to.

"What is your *problem*, man?" I demanded, trying to sound angry rather than close to tears.

Kevin ran a hand through his hair, exhaled sharply, then looked up at me. His face was softer now but he still looked different, just like the day before on the bus. Just like he'd looked since school started, if I was honest with myself. Something had happened. Where was my friend? The person I knew?

"Look," he began, and from that very first word I knew it was going to hurt. "We... I don't think we should hang out so much anymore, okay?"

I sat there. My palms were sweating onto the crinkly material of my sleeping bag but I didn't move, didn't want to betray how I was feeling.

Kevin waited for me to say something. When it became apparent we were in a standoff, he sighed again.

"You're just... you're too close to me. People notice. Guys in class notice. They think–they say we're—"

"I'm not gay," I said, but it was just the first thing out of my mouth. I didn't know yet, hadn't had that special moment where I knew if I liked girls or guys, I just knew I liked *Kevin*, and at that very moment Kevin was tearing my heart out of my chest.

"It doesn't matter," Kevin said, waving a hand in the air like he was swatting away a fly. "They're calling us fags, they've been calling us that since school started up again this fall and I can't take it anymore. I could actually be popular if it weren't for this, you know? Until they started calling you my boyfriend I actually had a shot getting Christy Wilkins to the Halloween Dance."

"Who gives a shit about Christy Wilkins?" The words burst out of me like I'd been holding my breath the entire time he was speaking. Maybe I had.

"You're being selfish, Jason! You can have other friends, *we* just can't hang out anymore, until maybe they drop the whole gay thing—"

"I don't *want* other friends!" I said, and now I was sure he could hear the tears in my voice, they were threatening to spill and wouldn't *that* be fucking grand, he'd all but called me a faggot to my face and there I sat weeping like a little girl. I tried to turn the situation back to my stupid scary story, desperate for the distraction. "I didn't even tell you the best part about the Skinstealer, the part where you summon him like Bloody Mary—"

"I don't want to hear the rest of the story, Jason," Kevin said, and he sounded very tired, and at that moment I thought I could kill him. I really did.

I liked him. I liked him so much.

We stared at each other for what felt like a very long time. Finally I opened my mouth and even though I was sure I was about to start sobbing, what came out instead was, "Okay."

Relief flooded Kevin's face.

"Okay?"

"Yeah," I said, my voice seeming very far away and very small. "It's fine. This is the last one anyway. The last sleepover. It's fine. It was fun."

"It was," he agreed. I felt it again, the cold stab of hatred because I liked him and he was abandoning me, he was turning his back on me just like when I'd started to tell the Skinstealer story.

"It's fine," I said again.

"Cool. Thanks man. I know it sucks, but I bet if we don't walk home together, if we just kinda back off—"

"It's fine."

"—they'll back off too and maybe we can hang out again." He was settling back into his sleeping bag. He was going to sleep. He was going to sleep while I was breaking in two.

"Maybe," I echoed, and I pretended like I was going to sleep too, I rolled over in my sleeping bag and turned my back to him and Kevin said something else but I didn't hear him because my heartbeat was pounding thick in my ears and I'd already decided what I was going to do next.

It was really stupid. It was a dumb, stupid thing to do but I was angry and it wasn't supposed to work.

I waited until Kevin fell asleep, listened for his deep measured breaths, then slipped from my sleeping bag and tip-toed to the bathroom. I didn't switch on the light, and that was scary, but I didn't switch it on because you were supposed to do it in the dark.

I gripped the clammy edges of the sink to ground myself. I stared into the darkness where I knew the mirror was. I inhaled through my nose.

"Skinstealer skinstealer, come and steal my skin today. Skinstealer skinstealer, I wasn't using it anyway."

I said the stupid rhyme three times. It's what the kids at camp said you were supposed to do, if you were brave enough. It was supposed to be a dare. If you could do it, you were brave.

Then I did the last part.

"Kevin," I said, because you were supposed to say your own name. So he would know whose skin to steal.

It was stupid, like I said. But I stood there for a long time. I wanted the Skinstealer to come and scare Kevin, I wanted him to be scared by my story and I wanted him to pay just a little bit, maybe cry like I almost did. The idea felt good, like a warm heavy stone in the palm of my hand.

I wanted him to be scared because I was scared. I didn't have any friends now, no one on my shitty boat anymore, everyone thought I was gay and what if I actually *was* gay, what if they were right? It was all too much to take at once and I was fucking terrified.

The story wasn't clear on how the summoning was supposed to work. That's the problem with urban legends, I guess, they end up twisted and parts fall off and get lost, no one remembers how they got started in the first place. The Skinstealer was just supposed to come.

But of course he wouldn't, so I turned on the light and took a leak before going back to the bedroom.

The first thing I noticed when I opened the door was how dreadfully cold my room had become. I thought maybe the window was open, maybe Kevin had cracked it a little when I went to the bathroom, but Kevin hadn't moved from his sleeping bag.

The second thing I noticed was the dark form crouched over him.

My mouth fell open and a dry little gasp popped out. I couldn't have stopped it any more than one can stop their own heartbeat, but the form turned towards me with a sharp snap of their head.

He was beyond skinny, beyond gaunt – the angles of his face were severe, cheekbones standing out like rocky crags. His eyes were set deep in his head. The circles surrounding them were dark and puffy, painful looking. His thin lips curled out, giving them a grotesquely seductive pout. He was bald. Moonlight shone off the stretched-tight skin of his skull. He reminded me of the photos in our history books when we learned about the Holocaust.

Around his shoulders was something that resembled a quilt of many squares. The squares were uneven, different shades and textures. They faded as they reached his shoulders, as though those pieces were the oldest. Those looked like they would feel like paper if you could bear to touch them.

The Skinstealer's livery lips parted, revealing a crooked row of teeth that made me think of old tilted headstones in untended graveyards. He pointed at the Sharpied name on the sleeping bag where Kevin lay slumbering.

"Kev-iiiinnnnnnnnnn," he whispered, drawing out the last syllable. It was the most horrible thing I'd ever heard. I was afraid he'd never stop and the sound would drive me crazy.

"Yeah," I said when it finally did. "It's fine."

He grinned again. I think it was a grin. All those crooked, tilted teeth.

"Good little patches," he murmured, turning back to Kevin and releasing me from that hideous smile. "Good little patches for my blanket, he will make good little patches. He will be warm. He is not using it anyway." I couldn't see what he had but there was a quiet sound of metal on metal as the Skinstealer fished out some sort of tools and all at once I knew what was going to happen and I'm not going to lie to you, I'm not going to lie to myself because I can't, I was *happy* to hear those tools coming out of his bag because I liked Kevin and Kevin had hurt me.

Kevin never cried out. I don't know if he even woke up. The Skinstealer worked quickly and quietly, his bony fingers moving with the fluid ease of someone very good at what they do. Then the wet, slippery sounds started and everything began to grey at the edges and I fainted dead away just as he peeled a long flap of skin off of my best friend's limp, lifeless forearm.

I didn't see what happened after that because when I woke up, the Skinstealer was gone. Kevin was gone.

There was a small bulge under the sleeping bag, just near where it read "Kevin." Other than that my bedroom was just as neat as you please, no evidence that anyone had ever been there at all.

It was almost 2 in the morning and it was freezing outside but I took the bones to the woods that edged my backyard. It took me almost an hour to dig the hole but it wasn't too bad because the Skinstealer had made it easy, Kevin was in good little pieces and the hole didn't have to be that big to fit all his bones. I buried them deep. I did it like I'd been doing it all my life, then I went inside and washed off the shovel. I washed my hands. I took another leak and I went back to bed.

In the morning, when I woke up at 10am (customary for most Saturdays), I asked my parents if they knew where Kevin was.

I don't know if they ever found him. I guess not, since after we moved away we never heard anything from his parents again. His mother, clutching his sleeping bag where it still read "Kevin" in big Sharpie letters, wept to my mother and said she had been worried about him lately. Since school started he'd been moody, unlike his usual cheerful demeanor. She blamed herself for not seeing the signs. She thought he'd run away but she was sure he'd be back, eleven is such a difficult age for boys, their changing bodies and their confused minds. He had just turned eleven and he was going to come back.

I know you don't believe me but I never meant for it to happen. Kevin was my friend. I liked him.

I liked him so much.

I have to live with it every day, the fact that I killed my best friend because I was angry that fear had driven him away from me. I have to look at my face in the mirror and know what I did.

And each time I do, each time I grip the edges of my sink and stare deeply into my reflection, I have to stop myself from switching off the light and saying the words. The words that will make my bedroom dreadfully cold, will conjure the Skinstealer from whatever dark realm he exists in until he's called upon by someone stupid enough to issue a dare.

Because when I do, I know I'll say my own name this time.

IF I SHOULD SLEEP WITH A LADY
CALLED DEATH

She was young and beautiful but of course you already knew that. The professor-student affair is a tired old trope and a very specific picture leaps to mind when you hear it. Don't fool yourself by acting like you don't know what it is from the start: an English professor who's started to gray around the temples, who's still in okay shape for a guy his age, who's been considering buying a mid-life-crisis-mobile and ended up fucking one of his students instead.

Her name was Lisa and she pretended to be confused about the meaning of an E. E. Cummings poem. He knew she wasn't–the way her eyes lit up as he explained the narrator's acceptance for greater oblivion in the initial lecture was something a teacher doesn't miss. She knew exactly what the poem meant but she asked him to explain again, frowning prettily, tapping her finger on the line "seeing how the limp huddling string" and pretending to be just so confused by the whole thing.

It was adorable. It was a trap.

We'll spare you the details of how they got to the inevitable. Do you really want to watch those cliché scenes play out, him meeting her in a coffee shop for some "conversation", the two of them somehow finding our way to a local bar, his clumsy attempt to kiss her that fumbled at first but ultimately set this entire thing into motion?

Let's just skip to the good part.

At first they were both insatiable. It was nothing and then it was everything. His wife had shut him out long ago and now their bed was only for sleeping but he and Lisa melded their bodies together so sweetly that he never wanted to leave the hotel room. She was young, she was beautiful, she moved in ways that had him thinking about her days later in the most inappropriate of places. Erections beneath his desk in the lecture hall became a natural occurrence. And it was as if she *knew*... Lisa would catch his eyes at the exact moment his mind played along their steamy indiscretions. She would smile. He would feel the heat of a blush creep into his scalp and try to find his place in the lesson plan.

Yet as the affair drew on something changed in her; there was a hunger inside Lisa the professor couldn't touch, like a rabid dog that tries so desperately to drink but can't keep water down. The young beautiful girl began to fall apart at the seams. She clung to him, wept when he tried to go long after he should have, threatened to leave him and told him she'd die without him in the same breath.

The beautiful ones, they're often the most broken inside. Their pretty masks hiding shattered glass. Of course, you already knew that.

One sleepy afternoon, in the middle of making love, him on top and her beneath... she looked him straight in the eyes and clawed her nails down his back.

It hurt a little, but not a lot, so he kept pumping away, but then she did it again, harder this time. He told her to stop but she didn't; she arched her back, made a mewling sound of pleasure, and did it *again*.

She broke the skin, he actually *felt* it tear, and he shoved himself off of her as soon as the blood began to run down his back. Even as he pulled away she was begging him to stay, she was so close, she was almost there.

Looking over his shoulder, the mirror above the hotel dresser displayed ten incriminating marks: razor-thin slashes oozing blood like thick red ink. They were unmistakable. They were evidence.

He was furious. He'd managed to stay under the radar until now but there was no way his wife wouldn't notice this, he would have to go to great lengths to hide it and as shitty as it was he didn't want to leave his wife. How else would he fit into this played-out stereotype if he did?

We all play our parts in the end.

Lisa cried. She pawed at him like a cat as he dressed, telling him she was sorry, she'd gotten carried away because it was so sexy, *he* was so sexy, she simply couldn't control herself. She crawled towards him and tried to unbutton his pants again.

He didn't hit her. That, he can say. In the moment he was so angry and he raised his hand like he might but he didn't.

Something changed in her face then, he saw it but didn't identify what it was. He didn't care. He was just so angry to be bleeding through his expensive shirt and wondering how he'd replace it before his wife saw.

There is power in blood. You already knew that.

Please, she said. Please don't go. I need you. More of you. All of you.

He left her there with money on the dresser for the hotel room. Like a whore. It wasn't nice. Maybe he wasn't a very nice guy, even though he always thought he was.

The end of the semester was around the corner so he cut ties with her. Lisa didn't need the help she'd come to him for in the first place, she had a solid A in the class even with missing the final. That girl really knew her poetry.

He didn't hear from her again, unless you count the cryptic message she left on her course review sheet; under the section "comments about the professor" she wrote: *Something which is worth the whole.* Cummings. Out of context, it made no sense. He decided it was her goodbye.

Summer rolled in with its big lazy clouds and simmering heat. His wife never noticed the claw marks on his back or, at least, didn't mention them. They healed over into scabs, then thin white scars, almost unnoticeable. Almost as if it had never happened at all. How easily we forget what was once our everything.

One night his wife rolled over in bed, looked him in the eye, and touched him in the way she hadn't in a very long time. They reconnected, quite literally. It was better than he'd remembered.

Maybe she knew about Lisa. Maybe she didn't. It didn't matter at first. Not until the worms.

You know how after it rains, when the sidewalk squirms with scores of slimy earthworms? The rain forces them out of the soil and they dumbly find their way back when it dries.

There hadn't been any rain. It was one of the driest summers on record, in fact, and the scorched soil needed the rain, but the grass went yellow and stiff without moisture. So you can imagine his surprise when, the morning after his wife and the professor made love, he went to the porch for the front paper and found worms.

There were only a handful, maybe 20 or so, but they were squirming all over the newspaper's protective plastic cover. He brushed them off, puzzled, and didn't give it a second thought. As he did with many things.

But they were back the next day. More this time. He swept them off the porch with an old broom and googled "how to kill earthworms" only to find hundreds of hippies telling him they were just part of the natural ecosystem and too special to be exterminated. He ignored their warnings. As he did with many things.

Later in the week he went to the fridge for a sandwich. It was leftovers, but really good ones, a pulled pork hoagie from a local hole-in-the-wall and it had fried pickles on it and his mouth was watering for the thought even though it was cold and a day old. He put it on a plate and got some chips and settled down with a book. He took a bite.

Spat it out at once.

Worms.

His stomach rolled as he stared at the hunk of bread, pulled pork, and about a dozen worms that had been neatly bitten in two when he took the first chew. He ran to the bathroom and vomited into the sink, unwilling to look at what had come back up.

When the professor went to the back porch for fresh air... more worms.

So many worms.

He could hardly see where the cement ended and his yard began. Like a thick blanket of sod that had been laid down to hide the grass rather than help it, a writhing layer of brainless little slimes. It seemed to breathe on its own. It seemed to move towards him.

It all happened so quickly, there had been none and now there were thousands, they were everywhere he turned. They floated in his coffee. They crawled out from between the couch cushions. They squirmed in every pair of shoes he owned. The worms were nothing and then they were everything.

Suddenly, and all at once, he understood.

When his wife came home one afternoon, he told her. Not about the worms, she couldn't see them anyway and somehow he knew that. The professor told her about Lisa and how he'd fucked her and left her and how he was sorry, for both of them, for all of them.

She said she'd take some time. He told her he needed that, too.

As he was drifting off to sleep that night, occupying one half of a bed that should've held two if not for his indiscretions, he heard it. A quiet squelching sound like rain boots in mud.

They were coming for him.

He tried to scream but he was stuck in that twilight state between dreams and reality; his limbs felt like they'd been packed with cement. He could do nothing but watch as the worms slowly squirmed their way into his room, a disgusting mass of brainless little bodies, becoming thicker and more substantial as it inched nearer to his bed. To him.

Darkness overtook the edges of his vision and as he crossed the threshold into oblivion he swore he felt them caress his face, a touch that would've felt tender without the slime.

When he woke up the next morning, alone, the worms were gone.

Of course they were.

The professor heard through the grapevine that not long after his nightmare about the worms — because that's what he'd convinced himself it was, a nightmare, a hallucination fueled by his guilt and grief — they found Lisa's body in her off-campus apartment. No one had heard from her since the semester ended and a concerned friend got the building's super to unlock the door.

She'd taken a bath and opened a vein and, well, that was that.

Except, of course, for the message scrawled in blood-red lipstick on the mirror, the one that got everyone talking, words that no one seemed to understand but the professor:

AN INCH OF NOTHING FOR YOUR SOUL.

12

GRACIE IS GONE

I am a good mother.

I made sure to read all the books when I was pregnant, knew what to expect and learned the business of being born. I wanted to be ready. I wanted to be prepared.

And I was. I brought her into this world and once she was here I made sure I knew how to take care of her, what to do when she cried, how to soothe her to sleep and feed her and change her. I took such pride in it. She was a part of me, a piece of my heart that somehow miraculously existed outside my ribcage. It was important to be ready. It was important to be prepared for whatever life threw at us because she was my baby girl and between my husband and me, she completed our family.

But nothing can prepare you for the heart-stopping moment, the sheer plummet of your guts as you open the door to your child's room and see, instead of a sweetly sleeping toddler, a tangle of empty sheets and a curtain flapping in the breeze.

You stare in disbelief. You try to will your child back into existence. Your mouth goes dry.

Then you begin to scream.

My husband found me on my knees in Gracie's nursery, sobbing, pointing helplessly to the crib. Saying her name over and over like a prayer. I had only put her to bed an hour ago but I always checked on her, made sure she was warm, made sure she had her stuffed lamb, made sure she was safe. And now she was gone.

Nothing can prepare you for the questions of police officers only doing their job. They have no idea how it's ripping your soul in two to describe your daughter in the most clinical of terms, noting any birthmarks or recognizable features because it may help bring her home but right now the things that made her special are just words scratched in pen in a tired cop's notebook. The pink footie pajamas she wore, an "identifying characteristic."

No one has written a book about what to expect from the sleepless nights where your cruel brain presents you with all the terrible things that could've happened to her. What it feels like to lie next to your husband, both of you awake and unspeaking, scenarios like child pornography and sexual abuse running through your head... there's no pamphlet that walks you through this.

Days went by. Gracie's crib remained empty. My heart broke every morning I woke and thought *I should check on the baby* only to realize all over again that she was gone.

Nothing can prepare you for the first time you realize your daughter might be gone forever.

There were press conferences. Flashes of cameras as they snapped photos of my stunned face while my husband spoke in slow, wavering tones, begging whoever had taken her to bring her back. Gracie's sweet little smile plastered on telephone poles, bus stop benches, the evening news. Candlelight vigils.

I am a good mother but I was not prepared for this.

Weeks went by. The posters declaring Gracie MISSING in big accusatory letters slowly began to fade and peel at the corners. Our neighbors, who had previously brought covered glass pans of casserole and cake because grieving parents cannot cook for themselves, they stopped coming around so often. *Gone forever*, my mind whispered. *Gone.*

And then we got the phone call.

A little girl matching Gracie's description had been found in a neighboring city, wandering the streets downtown with no shoes or socks. She was dressed in an oversized men's t-shirt and she was crying but she matched the description we'd given of our two-year-old daughter so could we come to the station to identify her, please?

My husband nearly crashed our car on the way to the police station. I held his hand and reminded him that it might not be her, we shouldn't get our hopes up.

But it was.

She was sitting on a police officer's lap, tears rolling down her cheeks as she chewed nervously on her fingers. My beautiful blonde little girl, my darling Gracie, sitting there like she'd never been gone at all. I scooped her into my arms and kissed her as my husband wept openly.

We took her with us, back to the bed she'd disappeared from. We cleaned her dirty little feet. Dressed her in warm, soft clothes. Cradled her and kissed her and told her we loved her.

She was different, somehow. She shied away from us as though she had no idea who we were. Her stuffed lamb held no interest for her. She was much quieter than before; her beautiful blue eyes would often unfocus and stare at the wall while we cooed and cuddled and tried to hug her back to normal.

God only knows what she went through.

A month after Gracie came back, a man came to our house. He knocked on the door and I answered, Gracie on my hip. I didn't recognize him.

He smiled, first at Gracie, then me.

He said, "So Gracie is home again, huh?"

I was confused. I asked him if he was a reporter, because those had finally stopped coming weeks ago, but he shook his head. He kept smiling, a smile I grew to like less and less the longer he stood there.

"Got yourself a happy ending, didn't ya?" he said, a strange lilt in his voice. "'Course you did. Everyone wants a happy ending. You know, though, sometimes? Sometimes people don't get one."

Gracie began to cry. I started to shut the door in his face but he stuck his foot inside, stopping me.

"How sure are you," he asked me, "that this is your daughter?"

He started to laugh. I know you'd like to hear that it was maniacal, the laughter of a crazed lunatic, but it wasn't, it was worse because it sounded so normal.

I closed the door again and again on his foot until he finally withdrew. I turned the lock and called the police, trying to soothe Gracie's frantic sobs. By the time they got to our house the man was gone, but his words echoed in my head for days.

How sure are you?

It was a sunny day. Gracie was napping contentedly on the picnic blanket I'd laid out so I could work in our garden. I couldn't bear to have her out of my sight so I brought her everywhere with me.

I was pulling weeds from the section where our herbs grew when I found the body.

An impossibly little body, badly decomposed. The face was a mangled mess. Maggots squirmed in the decay.

Next to it, a folded pair of pink footie pajamas.

Nothing can prepare you for this.

I buried it next to the mint and rosemary. First the pajamas, then the body.

Because you know what? He was right. I wanted my happy ending.

And I'm going to get it.

After all, I am a good mother.

13

BUBBLEHEAD ROAD

———

I got the first idea something was wrong when Mark wouldn't tell us what movie we were going to see.

"We're seeing 'Manhattan', right babe?" Barbara asked, flipping down the passenger side mirror to check her hair. "I love that Woody Allen. He just seems so... smart."

"You wouldn't know smart if it bit you in the ass," Mark replied easily. I hated it when he talked to her like that but Barb just gave him a babygirl pouty face.

"Don't be mean, babe, it's date night."

"I mean, it's not like I *want* smart to bite you in the ass." Mark chuckled a little at his own cleverness. "I like your ass just the way it is, cute and dumb."

Barb wasn't dumb, not really, but she went back to checking her hair as if he hadn't said anything at all.

I turned from my spot in the backseat of Mark's car to check the position of the sun on the horizon. It was getting dark, nearly past dusk, and I didn't really recognize where we were. Mark was Dennis's friend, not mine, and kind of slimy, so you can see why I'd be a little worried.

"Where are we going?" I asked Dennis. He shot me a grin and put a hand on my knee, jiggling it back and forth in a way that was meant to loosen me up.

"The movies, hon."

"No, I know that," I said. I was making a real effort not to sound scared or naggy but Mark was driving down this dark road I didn't know – way too many trees around for us to be going to the movie theater in town. Maybe we were going to a drive-thru I didn't know about?

"To see 'Manhattan', right babe?" Barbara said again.

"What movie *are* we seeing?" I asked Dennis, ignoring her.

"Don't get your panties in a twist, Pammy," Mark said over his shoulder. "Den, tell your chick to chill."

I didn't trust Mark as far as I could've thrown him but I trusted Dennis, so I put my hand over the one on my knee and made earnest eye contact with my boyfriend.

"Dennis, we're going to the movies, right?"

We'd been dating since sophomore year, we'd lost it to each other at prom, I knew him more than I knew any other person on the planet and that's why I was able to see in that moment that he didn't want to lie to me anymore. He started to, I think, but I gave his hand a little squeeze and he cracked.

"Mark, we can tell 'em now, can't we?" Dennis said.

I pushed his hand off my knee.

"Tell us what?" I asked. We made a left onto a road going into the woods, leaving behind the main road, and I twisted in my seat to sneak another look at the sun as it set.

"We better not be seeing that movie 'The Dark'," Barbara said. She was reapplying her lipstick now. "Looks like alien-horror-bullshit. Plus I hate scary stuff."

"You're not gonna be too happy with me then, babe," Mark snickered as he flicked on his headlights.

"Dennis, tell me what the hell we're doing," I said urgently. It was darker in here now that the thick-leaved trees were blotting out the last rays of the dying sun and I was starting to get nervous.

Barbara flipped up the mirror, tucking her lipstick back in her purse, and looked around as though she'd only just noticed where we were.

"Hey, you fucker, if you think I'm gonna do it in a creepy old place like this you're crazy!" She turned around to see me. "Where are we, Pam?"

"Ask your dumbass boyfriend," I spat, thoroughly out of patience. "He's the one driving."

"Pam," Dennis said, reaching for me again, but I shrunk away from him against the car door. I had no interest in his hand on my knee at that moment; all I wanted to do was go home.

"Mark, tell us where we're going or I swear to god I won't put out until after graduation." Barb emphasized this by crossing both her arms and her legs.

Mark sighed and slowed the car to a stop.

"Okay, Jesus Christ woman," he said, leaving the ignition running. He turned to face both Barb and the two of us in the backseat. "We're going to Bubblehead Road, it won't be that long and *then* we'll go see a fucking movie, any fucking movie you ladies want, okay? How's that sound?"

"Take me home," I said at once. If we hadn't already driven a mile or two deep in the woods I would've gotten out right then and there.

"Pam," Dennis said again. "It's not gonna be anything bad, I promise."

"You know what they say about that place! It's fucking haunted, or worse—"

"Oh, it's way worse than that," Mark said, grinning.

"You fuck," Barb snapped. She picked her purse up off the floor and hit him halfheartedly in the shoulder with it. "I told you hate scary shit! You heard Pam, take us home!"

"So you're saying you *don't* know the legend of Bubblehead Road?" Mark raised his eyebrows at us.

"I don't care about any legend of anything, I want to go see 'Manhattan'!"

Dennis put a tentative arm around me. I didn't move out of it, mostly because I was preoccupied by the fact we were in the woods where the light was quickly fading and I just wanted to go somewhere else.

"Pam, listen," he murmured in my ear. "Some of the guys on the football team, they gave us this stupid dare and we needed you to see us do it. They won't believe us if we said we did. We'll be in and out, I promise."

"I would've just lied for you," I hissed back.

"Yeah, but you're a terrible liar." He smiled at me, that smile that still made my stomach do acrobats, and wiggled a playful finger in my side. I laughed despite myself.

"What stupid shit did you two get yourselves into?" Barb demanded.

"It's easy-peasy baby," Mark said, reaching towards her so he could play with her long brown hair. "We go to the house at the end of Bubblehead Road, touch the front door, and leave. That's it. You two sexy ladies use this—" He picked up a Polaroid camera from the floor near his feet and dumped it unceremoniously in Barb's lap. "—snap a pic for proof, and all the guys owe us beer on graduation night."

"Let's get this over with," she sighed.

"Barb!" I tried to lean towards her and Dennis pulled me back into his arms.

"What? Let them do their stupid thing and then we can go to the movies, like Mark said." She tossed her hair back, picked up the camera. "But you're buying me popcorn. And soda. And any candy I want."

"Sure thing, babe," Mark said, grinning again. He put the car into gear and we continued along the road – Bubblehead Road.

"I didn't agree to this," I whispered to Dennis, whose arms had relaxed now that he saw we were back on track. "You're a real jerk for making me go along, you know, and not even telling me. I heard this place is dangerous."

"I'm sorry," he whispered back, but Mark's eyes were on me in the rearview mirror.

"What exactly did you hear, Pammy?"

I fucking hated it when he called me Pammy.

"I heard they took drugs," Barb said, like he'd spoken to her. "Everybody in the family, they didn't have much money so the government made 'em guinea pigs for cash and their heads got huh-YOOGE." She demonstrated this by miming an explosion over her skull. "When it went wrong they got dropped out here so they couldn't tell anyone else, government paid 'em off. Right babe?"

"You're stupid, babe," Mark said flatly.

"I heard they were just inbred hillbillies," Dennis offered. "They settled out here when they were pioneers and only married each other for years and years and years and now they're all—" He searched for the word, didn't find it, and shrugged. "—fucked up, I guess."

"Big heads, right?" Barb twisted in her seat again to look at us. I could see the dying light of the day reflected in her shiny lipstick.

"Yeah, big heads. Bubbleheads is what they call them."

"I heard they eat people," Mark said.

"Oh Jesus, Mark, that's disgusting." She swatted his shoulder lightly. I wanted to sock him in the mouth.

"It doesn't matter what I heard," I spat, suddenly furious with all of them. "It's getting dark and we're driving down this shitty road and it's – we don't know what's out there, Dennis, all this for a few beers?"

"There's probably nothing, Pam," Dennis assured me with a little squeeze of my shoulders.

"Then what's with these signs, huh?" Mark pointed at a crooked sign we were passing that read in big, black letters: NO TRESPASSING.

"Probably to keep out idiots like you," I said under my breath.

"Your chick, Den," he said, an undercurrent of warning in his tone.

Beyond him I could see the snaking stretch of road disappearing as it bent first one way, then another. The trees were getting thicker and it was getting darker and I couldn't believe my normally sweet, smart boyfriend was making me do this.

"Hey, he's right, there's another one," Barb said.

And another. And another.

The four of us lapsed into silence as we passed sign after sign bearing the same threatening message over and over: NO TRESPASSING. PRIVATE PROPERTY. NOTICE – TRESPASSING ABSOLUTELY FORBIDDEN. KEEP OUT.

NO TRESPASSING.

"I counted nine of them," Dennis said at last.

"Yeah, that means someone definitely doesn't fucking want us out here, so please turn around and let's go home," I begged.

"We're almost there, Pammy, Jesus." Mark's eyes met mine again in the rearview mirror. "I wanted to rile you girls up a little but come on, you know there's nothing out here. It's just a bunch of made-up bullshit. We'll be in and—"

"Shit, stop!" Barb shrieked.

The car lurched as Mark slammed on the brakes; Barb and I screamed, Dennis threw a protective arm across my chest to stop me from flying forward.

A moment of silence went by until Mark turned on Barbara.

"What the fuck, Barb, you trying to get us killed?!" he shouted.

"Why don't you watch the road, you stupid fuck," she countered breathlessly. "Something ran in front of the car, you almost hit it!"

"What was it?" I looked out my window but I didn't see anything, just trees, and I'd be damned if I was going to roll it down to look harder.

"I – I don't know, it moved so fast, it was just this dark shape—" Her pretty face began to twist like she was about to cry. "I changed my mind, Mark, I want to go home."

"Look, we're already here," Mark said, pointing at a white house just beyond the little stone bridge we were stalled at.

It looked like a two-story farmhouse but small, neat, kind of like a dollhouse I once had when I was a kid. A large double-level deck jutted from one side, a garage from another. White slats, blue shutters, poky little spiked fence. There wasn't anything wrong about it, nothing inherently creepy, but I still wanted to turn around and make the winding trip right back out of the forest before we lost the light completely.

"See?" Dennis said, giving my leg a comforting squeeze. "We'll be able to make the 9 o'clock movie. Promise."

We were already there. I couldn't say no. I couldn't make them stop.

"Okay, just go," I said, defeated. Mark stepped on the gas again and we crossed the bridge, his headlights flooding the front yard and bringing everything to a brilliant contrast.

"Turn your lights off!" Barb snapped.

Mark did, then turned around.

"You ready, Den?"

"Yeah." Dennis glanced at me and smiled. It was supposed to be a smile that said 'hey everything's fine' but he looked nervous. "You girls stay in the car, just take the picture when we get to the door and we'll be right back."

I tried to return his smile. I get the feeling mine didn't look too good either.

The guys hopped out of the car, shutting their doors quietly behind them. They left the engine running.

"Boys are so stupid," Barb said, but she watched Mark approach the house with nervous eyes. She was chewing on her lip and I don't think she knew it. The camera was poised, ready to snap the photo.

"Yeah," I agreed. I turned my own nervous eyes to Dennis, who was farther ahead than Mark. They were almost to the door, ready to touch it, when it swung open.

"Oh shit, oh god!" Barb was getting out of the car. Barb was getting out of the car!

"What are you doing?!" I said in a harsh whisper, but she was already gone, camera forgotten, running like an idiot towards her equally idiotic boyfriend who'd gotten us in this mess.

For a moment my lizard-brain insisted I get in the front and drive away. You know, that primal part of yourself that reacts only on pure animal instinct, bent on one thing: survival. Sometimes your lizard-brain knows what it's doing.

I hesitated, then got out of the car too, hoping I'd see all three of them just standing there, safe and sound.

And there they were. They *were* actually just standing there, together at the front door of the little white house, talking to a very normal-looking woman. I blinked a few times to be sure this was what I was seeing before walking towards the house, the car rumbling its engine behind me.

"We're really sorry," Barb was saying as I got closer.

"You're kids," the woman said amiably, wiping her hands on her apron. She was plain-faced, but smiling, and that was good. "Kids get up to all sorts of shenanigans. 'Specially right before summer. Like something gets inside 'em and makes 'em crazy." She turned her smile on me as I approached. "H'lo. You with these ones?"

"I am," I said. When I was by his side I grabbed Dennis's hand, hard, relieved everything was okay and furious with him all at once.

"Pretty girls," the woman said. "I never had no girls, just boys. You girls keepin' these boys in line?"

"Apparently not very well," I said, then laughed breathlessly. "We're so sorry, we didn't mean to trespass, we were just—"

"Oh, they already told me." She put her hands on her hips in a way that reminded me of my own mother when she had reached the end of her patience. "Silly stories. Aren't you too old for stories?"

"Yes, ma'am," Dennis said. The woman turned her smile on him and it grew warmer. Parents liked Dennis. "And we'll be going now. Get out of your hair."

"Yeah, sorry," Mark added needlessly.

"No worry," she said, waving a hand at us. "You didn't cause any trouble. Least had your music down. Can't tell you how often I come out here to godawful noise, devil rock music and screeching tires. You all had the sense to be *quiet* about it."

"We won't bother you again," I said, tugging on Dennis's arm to show him we should get the hell out while the getting was good. "It's getting dark, but it was nice meeting you—"

"Just tell those other kids that you didn't find nothing," the woman said, not unkindly. "The less of you out here, the better."

"You got it." Barb was also pulling on Mark, trying to make him move, but he was still standing there like he had missed something. "*Now*," she added, and finally he turned away from the little white house.

"Have a good summer," the woman called after us, "and stay out of trouble, you hear?"

"We will!" I shouted back.

When we were all in the car, I started laughing. Not quite hysterically, but in that scary way when you're not sure you can stop.

"Just a nice lady," I said between giggles. "A nice lady in an apron! You guys had me scared shitless!"

"When the door opened, I thought you were going to *die*," Barb said, her eyes wide and serious.

"She's watching us," Mark said.

We looked at the house, a good distance away now that we were in the car, and saw he was right. The woman was standing in the doorway, not much more than a silhouette from where we sat, but definitely watching.

"She wants to make sure we're leaving, asshole, let's go," Dennis said irritably. He was embarrassed, I could tell. I rubbed my palm over his back in soothing little circles.

"We didn't touch the door," Mark complained. He was trying to turn the car around with what little room he had on the stone bridge. "We didn't get a picture, you left the camera here."

"Who gives a shit?" Barb demanded. She regarded him for a moment with obvious distaste before folding her arms and looking out the window. "Forget the movie. Just take me home."

"If you're going to be a bitch about it—"

"Just take her home, Mark," Dennis snapped.

"Guys," I begged, my fit of laughter finally subsiding, "please, I have a headache, let's just—"

Then we heard it, a high warbling sound piercing through our argument. It sounded like a mix between a cat's yowl and a child crying 'ow!' – plaintive, keening, otherworldly.

We sat in stunned silence.

"What the fuck was—" Mark began, and we heard it again.

"Go, Mark," Barbara whispered after the last cry had echoed away.

He turned to look at Dennis, eyes wild.

"I told you there was something out here, man," he said excitedly. "Look, she went inside, let's just go back and see what it is—"

"Why the fuck would I want to see what it is?" Dennis demanded, incredulous.

"Okay, screw you then, I'll go do it." Mark opened his car door and hopped out. Barb made a strangled little sound of protest but didn't move. "Take the picture, Barb!"

"It's too dark," she said miserably.

The howl came again. It was nothing I'd ever heard before – terrible and yet somehow melodic, like the way the sirens must've sounded to Greek sailors.

"Dennis," I said, helpless.

"I know, I know..." He craned his neck, trying to catch a glimpse of Mark through the rear window as he walked back towards the white house.

"That stupid shit," Barb whimpered.

The three of us waited, Mark's car idling beneath us as we held our breath.

After what seemed like an eternity, I heard Mark scream.

Dennis was out of the car in a flash, running towards the sound of his friend's cry for help. Barb started weeping.

"He's dead, the Bubbleheads got him, he's dead," she managed through her sobs.

"I'm sure he's fine," I said, trying to see where they both were. Dennis was a vague blurry form in the quickly darkening dusk; Mark was nowhere to be seen.

Suddenly – unexplainably – I heard Mark laughing.

Barb and I looked at each other, made equals in our confusion. His laughing went on and on and for a manic moment I thought he'd gone mad but then I heard him yell:

"It's a stupid bird! A dumb fucking bird!"

I got out of the car, moving quickly towards where I saw them hunched over, about 15 feet away from the house.

"What's going on?" I whispered angrily.

"Mark kicked a bird," Dennis said.

As I got closer I saw it, the thing sprawled out on the ground near Mark's feet. It looked like a turkey until I saw that it wasn't a turkey, not at all, it was something far grander than that – something shimmering with iridescent colors and thick, luxurious feathers.

Its long elegant neck was stretched out in an expression of delicate surrender. As though it were saying, "Yes, you've won, lay your weapons down."

I stared at it, the little flourishes on its head and the larger ones on its rump, and finally said, "Mark, you killed a peacock."

"No way," he said immediately.

Dennis crept closer and squinted in the dusk's low light.

"She's right, man, it's a fucking peacock." He turned back to us, a baffled expression on his face. "Where did this thing come from?"

Almost as if on cue, we heard a more subdued version of the alien howl that had startled us in the car; a gentle yoo-yoo-yoo sound, like they knew one of their own had been murdered in cold blood.

"Is this a peacock farm?" I asked, bewildered.

A chorus of strange coos seemed to answer my question.

"Maybe that's what ran in front of the car." Dennis looked around, squinting, trying to see the other peacocks in the fast waning light. "You didn't have to kill it, man."

"So what," Mark scoffed. "It attacked me, what the fuck was I supposed to—"

And above the cooing, the plaintive mourning of birds in a foreign tongue, another sound interrupted him: a soft, hiccupping sort of cry.

It was quiet, but powerful. The kind of crying you do alone in your bedroom when you know someone's just outside and you can't break quite yet.

"Is that Barb?" Mark asked, already backing away.

"I don't think so," I whispered. I felt stuck to the earth where I stood. To move, I thought, would mean my certain death.

From beneath the steps of the little white farmhouse, a figure emerged, creeping on all fours towards us. It was small, but gangly, limbs hanging limply as it crawled along the grass.

Its head was huge.

Around where the jaw must've been was normal, sure, but from there it ballooned up, swollen like a ripe harvest pumpkin.

It was weeping.

"Don't...move," Dennis whispered. Mark kept backing away; I could hear sticks snapping beneath his feet as he went. I didn't need the suggestion, I couldn't have moved if I'd been ordered to. I was paralyzed with fright – surely I'd read that somewhere before and thought it some kind of flowery metaphor but it was true, you could be so scared that fear froze you in position like a fast-acting toxin.

The shadow crept closer, nearly to us now, and in the last shreds of the day's light I could see it was a boy – a little boy, maybe only 10 or 11. His head was grotesquely formed, yes, but his face was just a boy's face, streaked with tears. I noticed with dull fascination that he was wearing a little button-up sweater over corduroys, a snappy little ensemble to say the least. His knees were grass-stained.

The three of us stared at him as he tenderly lifted the limp peacock from the ground. He sat on his haunches, rocking slightly back and forth, and began to cry harder. He pulled the dead bird to his chest and wailed helplessly.

"You killed his pet, Mark," I whispered, swallowing back my own tears.

"It attacked me." Mark was coming closer now. I could hear him as he approached me from behind. I turned on him furiously, the panic lifting at last.

"Tell him you're sorry."

"It attacked me," he said again, but he wasn't really hearing me, he was staring at the little boy as he rocked on his heels and wept for his lost friend.

I couldn't stand it anymore, watching him cry like that. Very slowly, I approached the boy, careful as if he were a butterfly that could be startled and flutter away. When I was close enough I dropped to a knee.

"We're very sorry about your bird," I said softly.

He didn't look at me but I saw his hands sink deeper into the iridescent blue-green feathers as he hugged it, hard.

"Do you want us to talk to your... mom?" I looked at Dennis and shrugged, hoping I was right and the plain-faced woman we'd met earlier was the boy's mother. "We can talk to her, if you want."

"Fuck that, I'm getting out of here," Mark said, then snapped his fingers. "The camera! Oh, shit, I'm getting a picture of this freak!"

"Mark!" I snapped my head up to look at him but he was already gone, running back to the car for his Polaroid. This was enough – more than enough – and I wouldn't let it happen, I'd let too much happen already. "Dennis, do *not* let him take a picture, I am so god damn serious."

Dennis nodded and headed off in Mark's direction. I looked back and found the little boy watching me with wet brown eyes. His cries had tapered to sad sniffles but he was still rocking back and forth.

On impulse, I placed my hand gently on his little sweatered shoulder.

"I'm sure he was a good bird," I said softly. He gave a shuddering sigh and nodded.

I tried to smile. There was a hot lump in my throat and I forced it down; it was like swallowing a rock. All this for a few beers.

For a moment I didn't say anything. I just let him sit there, my hand on his shoulder, his dead peacock in his lap, trying to make sense of what this loss meant – what it could possibly mean that the bird wasn't moving and would never move again, never make its alien *yoo-yoo-yoo* sound that was probably music to this little boy's ears.

Then I heard footsteps. Mark was coming back, Dennis on his heels.

"I said no way," Dennis was hissing.

"Shut the fuck up, this is ten times better than a stupid picture of us touching the door!" Mark trotted up and towered over me, the Polaroid camera in his hands. "Move, Pammy, I'm gonna snap a pic of the Bubblehead."

I let go of the boy's shoulder, who was staring up at Mark with an expression of fear and confusion, to turn and block him from view.

"You're *not* taking a picture of him so you can show it off to your locker room buddies," I whispered fiercely. "You already killed his pet, Mark, just leave him alone."

"Pammy, I've about had it with your smart mouth tonight," Mark said, just a little too loudly. "If Dennis won't shut you up then I will. Move your ass."

I began to straighten with the intent of taking the camera away from him when he shot a hand out and shoved me, hard. Caught off guard and off-balance I went tumbling backwards into the little boy and his bird.

It all happened very fast:

Dennis grabbed Mark by the collar of his shirt and began to wrestle with him, trying to get Mark's head in a chokehold. Mark dropped the camera; it went off with a flash and a mechanical whirring noise. For an instant we were all painted in brilliant white light, a terrible portrait of grimaced, ugly faces.

I yelled a wordless sound as I hit the ground. The little boy began to really sob now, heavy piercing cries that bordered on screams.

I turned on my hands and knees to make sure he was all right. He looked okay, the bird looked okay (although still very dead), but before I could say something to make him calm down a cracking report sliced through everything else.

"NOT MY BOY!" someone screamed behind us.

Ears ringing, I whipped around to see the woman – the same plain-faced woman who'd turned us away with a smile and a kind admonition – standing on the steps of her house, pump-action shotgun in hand.

She wasn't smiling now. Her eyes were wild, the eyes of a mad grizzly bear protecting its cub. She cocked the shotgun, sending the spent shells flying, and leveled it at her shoulder.

It all came together at once in that terrifying way when your brain works faster than you thought possible – or perhaps you have your lizard-brain to thank – this was the boy's mother, she was not as she had seemed, and we only got one warning shot.

"Run!" I screamed, struggling to my feet.

Dennis released Mark and bolted towards the car. I could hear Barb inside, screaming. I lost my footing briefly but soon I was on my way too; I looked over my shoulder to see Mark on his hands and knees. I wasn't sure if Dennis had left him that way until I saw that he was grabbing for the camera.

"Leave it!" I shrieked, halfway to the car. Mark heard me and looked up – maybe that's what did it. Maybe that's all it took, that one second of hesitation. The woman took aim and fired the shotgun again.

Mark screamed in agony, crumpling over the Polaroid on the lawn in front of the small white house that was getting smaller as I ran. He was clutching his leg, still screaming, when I heard the woman bellow,

"Get 'em, boys! For your brother!"

I didn't know what that meant and I had no intention of sticking around to find out. We scrambled to the car, Dennis in the driver's seat, me in the back, Barb still wailing in the passenger seat.

"You left him, you left him!" she was shrieking.

"Drive, Dennis!" I twisted in my seat to look through the back window. Mark was still on the ground, grabbing his buckshot leg, screaming either in pain or for us to come back.

I was still watching him, my heart hammering in my ears, face hot with the rush of panicked blood, when I saw them come out of the woods.

Some of them had no legs and dragged themselves along the grass with thick, muscular forearms. Some had uneven limbs that swung back and forth as they lumbered across the lawn. Some had the same huge head I'd seen on the little boy, swollen to near impossible sizes.

They descended upon Mark and the screaming evolved into something beyond screams, a strangled tangled noise of pure animal panic and pain.

Barb heard this – did not see it – and began making the same shrill cry over and over like a dog that's been kicked.

"Go go go for the love of fucking god Dennis just drive!" I cried.

Dennis stomped on the gas. We were mostly turned back around towards the road but he had to do some maneuvering to get us pointed the right way on the little stone bridge. While he did Barb screamed and I pounded the passenger side window, urging him to hurry, hurry, please fucking hurry.

Gravel spat out from under our tires when he finally got us straight. There was the squeal of burning rubber and then we were off, barreling down the narrow winding road at breakneck speed.

"Mark, we left Mark, they got Mark, the Bubbleheads got Mark," Barb shrieked before dissolving into unintelligible gibbering.

We were going fast, too fast – each turn was nearly a miss, the car threatening to spin off the road or flip end over end. I kept looking through the back window to see if they'd followed us. I was sobbing uncontrollably but lizard-brain was in charge by then and it was almost like I was out of my body, regarding the situation with a sort of cool detachment. If we could get out of the woods, if they didn't follow us, everything would be okay.

We were nearly there, the trees were beginning to clear so I said, "I think we lost them—"

Just then I heard the sound of crunching metal and Dennis screaming. I whirled around to see one of them on the hood of the car; he looked like the boy's big brother with an enormous, grotesque head of his own, and I had only time to see two things before he began to bash the windshield with both fists: he was grinning, and he was wearing corduroys.

Dennis turned the wheel wildly from side to side, trying to shake the man off the hood, but it was no use – he was incredibly strong and well-planted, using his ropy muscled arms to smash again and again, causing the glass to splinter and crack beneath him.

Suddenly I felt my whole body seize forward. A bolt of pain went through my neck like nothing I'd ever felt before and, in the midst of Dennis and Barb's screams, everything went black.

I don't know how long I was out. When I woke up it was still dark; my entire body ached unbearably.

When I could force myself to sit forward, wiping the dried blood from my eyes, I saw what had happened. I remembered everything all at once: Bubblehead Road, the dead peacock, the little boy. Mark, that idiot, going back for the camera.

The car had crashed headlong into the trunk of a huge old tree. In the front seat, Dennis and Barb were unnervingly still.

Before I could lean forward to check on them further, I heard a rustling in the woods outside the shattered passenger window. Gingerly, I turned my head to see what it was, fearing more of the brothers.

It was the little boy, creeping along in his corduroy pants. The look on his face, his tiny face, the miserable eyes beneath the bulging head... I'll never forget it.

He didn't speak but I could almost hear him saying, "This is what happens."

Not an accusation. Not a threat. Just a sad, simple statement: this is what happens.

Suddenly his face was awash with lights of red and blue. His eyes widened and he began to scamper away, then thought better of it. He hurried to the car and dropped something in my lap through the devastated remains of the passenger window.

Then he was gone, scuttling away into the woods, back to his mother's house where his dead bird waited to be buried.

I tucked what he'd given me into my pocket as the lights got brighter and I started to lose consciousness. When the darkness crept into the corners of my vision I had enough time to hear "Stay calm, miss, don't move—" And then I was gone again.

I spent three weeks in the hospital, first for the car crash injuries, then because I'd been babbling after my surgery about monsters in the woods. They kept me for psychiatric evaluation, but by then I'd learned to keep my mouth shut and was soon approved for release.

There was a memorial at school for Dennis, Barb, and Mark. I didn't go. I couldn't bear the talking, the rumors, the classmates whispering about how when they found Mark's body it was little more than shredded meat and bone. Attacked by a mountain lion, some said, but others said much worse because it was the truth and they didn't even know it.

As for what the boy gave me, I don't know where it went. Maybe when they stripped me in the ambulance someone saw it and threw it out. Maybe they thought it was a prank. Or when they saw it, they couldn't reconcile with themselves what it really was, so it had to be destroyed.

Maybe the government has it. I don't know.

But I wish I still had it, because the boy meant for me to. It was meant as a warning. A permanent reminder of what monstrous things we can do when we don't know how our actions can hurt others, set in motion a terrible domino effect that leaves the lives of those involved forever damaged beyond repair.

So every day I try to picture it in my mind, keep the image sharp and crisp to honor what that little big-headed boy tried to teach me on an early spring night in 1979: a Polaroid of me as I fell backwards, pushed by Mark in an attempt to get his prized shot.

I'm drenched in white light. My teeth are pulled back in a grimacing sneer. My hands, windmilling as I tried to stop myself from falling, look like claws. My long dark hair is fanned around my head in a grotesque halo.

Behind me, clutching his dead bird, just about to start wailing, is the little boy. He's looking right at me. He's absolutely terrified.

Because I look like a monster.

14

LET'S BEGIN AT THE END

It's not where one would normally begin. Obviously. But that's what I like to think about. A lot. It's something definable, a concept that in and of itself is both totally clear and completely unknown. I think it's something beautiful.

That instant — it's what I think it is, an instant — where something is first there and then gone. Where has it gone? And why? I take these questions and wrap them around myself, entwine them through my fingers, keep myself warm beneath them.

Polite society is not supposed to focus on "the end." Rather, the middle, the boring part, the bologna of the sandwich, the long dry stretch of desert between birth and death. We're all supposed to just pretend that we don't think about it. How fucked is that? To deny something buried so deep within us it's practically part of our DNA? To act like the most important thing is whether we make enough money to buy a minivan?

No. Not me.

I think about it a lot.

I think about what it would be like if I did it, actually held a blade to the place where blood runs so precariously beneath skin. Would I be afraid? Exhilarated? Could I actually make that final move and see, at last, what the end looks like?

I think about my wife. How would she react? Would she be able to comprehend what she was seeing, what I was doing, the blade in my hand, the desire in my eyes? The longing for the end? Would she scream? Would she fight me? Or would she let me go, unwilling to believe I could follow through?

What would her face look like as I slit her throat?

I think it would be beautiful.

I think about it a lot.

And I bet you do, too.

15

WE FIND OURSELVES INFESTED

I've been texting our landlord ever since I heard the noises. At night, when we're almost asleep, we can just barely catch the scuttling sound as they hurry across the hardwood floor, disgusting little bodies clicking and clacking like dry bones in the darkness.

My text messages started politely enough – "Hey Jack, I think we might have a bug problem, could you look into that for us?" – but when he didn't respond I've had to grow more aggressive.

"Jack, we're infested. We need an exterminator and that's YOUR responsibility as a landlord. Can you PLEASE get one hired and sent over SOON? Thanks."

I hope the capitalized words and that stony thanks-with-a-period-at-the-end will be enough to convince him but all I've heard so far is, "Yeah sure looking into them now."

Yeah. Sure.

Marnie says the roaches are getting louder every night but sometimes Marnie exaggerates for effect. I love her but she can be a total pill.

"Last night I woke up and there was one on my pillow," she says this morning. "I screamed and swatted it away but I don't think I killed it. Those things are fucking impossible to kill, you know, I watched a National Geographic video on YouTube about it."

I dump the used coffee pod into the trash and brace myself for more. With Marnie, there's always more.

"Oh yeah?"

"Yeah," she says enthusiastically around a mouthful of granola bar. "They can survive a nuclear blast—" She says "nucular," not nuclear. "—they've been around for like three million years longer than humans, and when they mate the male excretes this sticky stuff—"

My appetite is in serious danger of being ruined. I change the subject.

"I didn't hear you scream last night," I cut in before I can hear what the sticky stuff is for.

Marnie stops and frowns.

"No?"

"No." Distraction successful. I peel a banana and scarf it down, hurrying as usual. I've been getting less and less sleep since we first noticed the disgusting bugs but you bet my boss is sick of my lateness and won't take roaches as an excuse. I dump the peel in the trash can.

"I'm pretty sure I screamed, Jessica," Marnie says thoughtfully, staring at the half-eaten granola bar in her hand. "I felt it right next to my head, next to my *face*, and I screamed and swatted it away."

I'm already tugging on my shoes and halfway out the door. I tell her fine, she screamed, whatever, I don't care, goodbye, have a good day. Then I'm down the hall and on the way to my car, away from Marnie's steadily irritating voice and the sound of cockroaches moving in the shadows that I've come to fear is constant.

When I get home from work it is suddenly, jarringly clear that Marnie didn't leave the house today. She is sitting in the living room, all the lights off, watching what must be the National Geographic video she mentioned earlier on our television. Wrapped in so many blankets – what looks like all the extra blankets in the apartment – she's barely visible, a Marnie-shaped lump. Her knees are pulled up beneath her chin and she's staring, slack-jawed, as roaches blown up to gargantuan size trundle back and forth across the screen.

"Marnie?" I say as I kick off my shoes at the door. "Did you look for work today?"

"Couldn't," she says simply. This one-word reply is strange for her but I'm wondering if she feels bad about skipping out on job-hunting so I push further.

"How come?"

"No paper," she says, gesturing with a limp hand towards our printer. "No résumé because we're out of...paper." The whole time she's staring at the television. Her face is lit up with this creepy blue glow and she reminds me of one of those kids whose parents never make them go outside to play.

Marnie's been out of work for a while now. I think it's starting to get to her. I tell her it's not a big deal, not really, but I can't support her for much longer and I'm pretty sure she knows that.

It's Friday and I don't want to think about this stuff right now. I just want to relax. I drop my purse on the couch. My eyes aren't adjusting to the darkness of the apartment, so I reach towards the switch and flip on the living room light.

Marnie lets out a shriek that sounds like the cats that mate in the alley outside my bedroom window at night.

"Turn that shit OFF!" she cries, and I do, as fast as a reflex.

A moment goes by where we just stay still, both of us shocked and startled by what happened.

"Sorry," Marnie mumbles at last. "My...eyes hurt. Allergies, maybe." She turns towards me from her nest of blankets on the couch, her mouth turned down at the corners. "Sorry, Jessica."

I tell her it's fine yet I can't help but notice how it seems like she's faking that look, like she's trying to form her face into the expression the way an alien would after studying tapes of human emotion.

I tell her it's fine but it's not, not really, I think she's starting to crack under the pressure of her unemployment so I go quietly to my bedroom because I can't stand to spend the rest of my night in the dark next to her.

Tomorrow, I think, I will talk to her about her state of mind. I'll see how she's feeling, and maybe we'll go to lunch. Marnie may be a handful but Marnie is my friend, so we'll figure this stuff out together. But that's tomorrow. Tonight I need to get some rest. I close the bedroom door behind me and settle into bed with my Kindle. I try not to notice the skittering sounds of roaches in the walls.

I check my phone for a text from Landlord Jack but there's nothing. I type "EXTERMINATOR NOW" in the message box, then erase it. I don't like confrontation, not even over the phone, so I give myself one more day. If he hasn't fixed this by Sunday, I'll really let him have it.

I wake up late on Saturday. Way later than normal but I've missed too much sleep these past few weeks so it feels good, like I got what I needed over the course of a single night. I stretch, crack my neck, and abruptly freeze in place when I spot the long parade-line of cockroaches marching across my bedroom floor, following the trim against the wall like a beaten path.

I resist the urge to scream and instead turn on the lamp next to my bed. All at once they scatter, darting in every direction like a firework exploding in the sky. Within seconds they're gone, hidden under the bed and in corners and behind the closet as though they never existed.

But they did, because I saw them, and I'm sick of this bullshit.

My hands are shaking as I make coffee in the kitchen, one hand shoving a mocha pod into the maker, the other jabbing out the text I'd intended to send the night before. "EXTERMINATOR NOW," I type again, and this time I actually hit send.

The coffee comes out hot, fragrant. This is good. I hold the mug with both hands, soothed by its warmth as I take long, slow sips. Jack will get back to me, of this I'm sure, and we will get the roach problem taken care of. No one can ignore a text in all-caps.

It's late, almost 11:30am, but I don't see Marnie anywhere. She must still be asleep. I finish my coffee at the kitchen table, checking Twitter and Facebook on my phone while I wait for a response from Jack.

Noon comes and goes. I watch Marnie's door, expecting her to come out at any moment, but she doesn't; soon I'm overwhelmed by the need to wash the grease from my hair and the sleep from my eyes. I leave my empty coffee cup in the sink and go down the hallway to her room, rapping my fingers on the closed door.

"Marnie?" I call softly, not quite wanting to wake her but also thinking hey, you lazy ass, get out of bed. "I'm jumping in the shower, Marnie, that okay with you?"

Silence. I wait a courteous thirty seconds before shrugging and heading to the bathroom, eager to surround myself with hot water and steam. I don't think there are cockroaches in the bathroom, not yet anyways – I haven't seen them there, but the little fuckers are so good at hiding I can't be sure.

I'm out of the shower, wrapping my wet hair in one of those mini-turban things when I hear a strange sound just outside the bathroom. I keep the door closed and locked when I shower, a bad habit I know – it can lead to black mold, but what the hell, we're already infested with roaches so what's a little mold in the face of total privacy? – but beyond the door I can hear this strange sound, munching, slurping, almost like a dog rooting through its bowl of food for something better even though all that's there is a pile of kibble.

Something tells me to be quiet, be careful, so I open the door slowly, just a crack to see what's out there, and why should I do it so slowly? Why should I be so careful? I'm not sure, it's something in my gut that tells me to do this so I do, and as the door finally opens enough to allow me a sliver of vision into the apartment I can see Marnie crouched over the trash can, shoveling handfuls of garbage into her mouth.

I don't mean that in a cute way, like she's eating junk food, I mean it in the very literal sense of the word: she is eating *garbage*, banana peels and fruit rinds and discarded yogurt straight from the plastic container. I watch her scoop the pink sludge greedily into her mouth, then drop the cup in search of more to devour.

I just stand there, staring at her through the crack in the bathroom door, my gorge rising as Marnie eats more and more from the trash. At some point she finds a coffee pod – the mocha one I'd made that morning – peels back the lid, and dumps the damp grounds straight down her throat.

I wait for her to stop but she doesn't, she's digging in deeper with both hands; I shut the door as quiet as I can. I think for a few minutes but I'm not sure what to do – in the past we've had some heart to hearts but there's nothing in my hey-Marnie-let's-not arsenal for this – so I just wait until the slurping, chewing, chomping grows quieter and finally fades away all together. Only then do I dare to stick my head outside and confirm Marnie's not in the kitchen anymore. She's shut herself in her bedroom again, and I note with dull horror that the parade-line of cockroaches I'd seen in my own room this morning is now slowly marching under her the crack of her closed door, one by one by one.

Lunch plans are, obviously, cancelled. I have no appetite and after the way she gorged herself like a pig on slop I can't imagine Marnie can be very hungry either. I alternate between waiting in my room with an old can of ant-killer and hovering outside hers, trying to figure out how to breach the subject of her bizarre behavior. Do I pull some Dr. Phil shit and try to get her to admit it on her own? Pretend like I didn't see anything and ask if she's been feeling well lately? Or just cut to the chase and say "Why the fuck are you eating our garbage, you lunatic?"

Before I can choose any of these not-so-stellar options I hear Marnie's voice. Our walls are paper thin (I'm truly beginning to regret moving into this piece of shit apartment) so most of our time is spent filling the place with sound: television, music, anything to keep from hearing what the other person is doing every minute of the day.

I've never wanted to eavesdrop before but I can hear her muttering – to herself, right? It's got to be to herself – and I find myself pressing an ear to the shared wall between our rooms.

"Warm," she's saying in a low, strange voice, "warm and nice, warm and *dark*. Thank you. Thank you for the warm dark place."

This is all it takes for me to consider calling a psychiatric hotline yet she goes on.

"More will come," Marnie says. "More and more. Need more dark. No light. All dark. Get rid of light. And STOP LISTENING TO ME!"

The last part comes as a shriek right next to my ear; I almost scream myself and jerk away from the wall. My hands are trembling, my heart is in my throat. She startled me good – how did she know I was listening?

I glance towards my door to see if she'll burst in but all I see is a lone cockroach braving the bright afternoon to stare at me from the floor, its antennae moving in a slow, sure rhythm: up, down, up, down.

I pick up the can of expired ant-killer and shake it but the rattle-clatter sends the roach skittering back under the door and into the hallway. I check my phone desperately for a text from Landlord Jack. No dice.

Enough is enough. I can only deal with one problem at a time and the roaches can be handled easier so I call Jack and wait impatiently as the phone rings, my legs tucked up tight under me. I have the strange itchy sensation like when you've just caught a bug crawling on you even though I don't think there are any more roaches in my room (right now).

It rings and rings and rings and Landlord Jack never picks up.

There's a moment where the silence in the apartment seems electric, almost crackling, and I get this wild impulse to jump up and lock my bedroom door – which is exactly what I do, just as the knob begins to rattle beneath my hand.

"Jessssssssica," Marnie says, the 's' in my name coming out in a slow hiss, "Let me in, Jessssssssica, I want to talk to you."

"I'm getting ready to take a nap," I blurt without thinking. "Do we have to talk right now? Because I'm getting ready to take a nap, so, you know, I'm about to take a nap."

A slow tap-tap-tap of fingernails on the door.

"Jessssssssica, can't we jusssst talk for a minute?"

I look down to see one, two, three cockroaches creeping under the door. In a manic moment of disgust I stomp down on each of them – one, two, three – and I swear I hear Marnie hiss again. The roaches leave cake-batter smashes on the hardwood.

"No, I'm pretty tired." I'm already reaching for the pile of dirty tee shirts in my hamper; I grab a handful and shove them under the door, blocking the entrance for any more curious cockroaches. "Just gonna lay down, get some shut-eye, you know?" Shut-eye? Am I a folksy old grandma? Clearly I'm not good at improvising but the tap-tap-tap only comes one more time before I hear her footsteps trailing away, towards the living room, and when Marnie is out of earshot I let out my breath in a relieved whoosh.

I dial Jack's number again. Still nothing. I shove more tee shirts under the door and hope that will stop the disgusting little fucks.

Marnie is clearly unhinged. I don't know what caused it – if I had to guess, her unemployment, and how that meant crawling back to her parents for more money, which she swore she'd never do – but something has happened, she is not in her right mind and she has been pushed over the edge. I would call her family but I don't have their number, and right now I'm honestly too scared to leave my room unless I know she's gone.

I check my phone again, uselessly. Nothing.

It doesn't occur to me to call anyone else for help because I'm still thinking of her as my roommate, my friend, my silly-simple Marnie who often takes things too far and doesn't know when to shut up. I'm still thinking of her as a normal person and maybe that's my problem.

It's almost 5pm and I'm starting to think maybe that nap is a good idea after all. I'm too afraid to go outside, I'm not sure where Marnie is and until I can pinpoint her exact location I just don't feel right leaving my room – it's sort of like that crackle I felt earlier, the one just before I locked my door. And who knows what would've happened if I hadn't?

I shove a few more pieces of laundry against the pile that's already crammed against the bottom of my door. Surely no bugs can get through there. The barrier of dirty clothes is at least a foot thick.

I give the tee shirt barrier a kick with my foot to be sure it's wedged firmly in place. It doesn't move.

I climb into bed, my head aching, my ears unconsciously pricked for Marnie's muttering voice to start leaking through the walls again. I tell myself I'll take one nap, that's all, just one nap, but as I lay down on the bed my bedroom door suddenly bursts open.

Marnie is standing there, grinning. I can see in the few seconds after that she's literally kicked my door down, the place on the frame where the lock goes is splintered and she's stepping inside, knocking aside my little barricade of soiled laundry like it's nothing.

"Remember when you told me I didn't sssscream, Jesssssssica?" Marnie says, that hiss seeping through her speech again. "You were right, I guesssss, I thought I'd ssssscreamed but you were right, I didn't sssscream because they told me to sssstop, they were already inssssside by then and even though I wanted to sssscream I didn't. Becausssse they didn't want me to."

I am scrambling for my phone to call 911, I don't know what's wrong with my roommate but there is most definitely something wrong, I will tell them she has a weapon even though she doesn't and someone will come to rescue me, I'm sure of it, they can stop her–

And it's then I notice the tiny antennae sticking out of her left ear, twitching violently like an epileptic's spastic fingers.

I freeze in place, one hand still reaching for my phone. I am trying to piece together what this means like an amputee staring at the spot where their limb no longer exists; all the information is right in front of me, everything I need to know, and yet none of it makes sense.

Behind her, a mass of roaches is surging over the pile of dirty laundry, covering my floor in a clicking brown blanket of shiny-shelled bodies. Together they're making a low hissing noise, not unlike how Marnie sounds when she says my name.

I watch in helpless terror as they invade my dresser, my nightstand, the edge of my bed. They crawl beneath the sheets and in the folds of my blankets. They file one by one into my pillowcases. Oddly enough, they leave a neat radius of space around where I sit – I'm trapped on my own bed by an army of cockroaches, and it feels like they're watching me.

No, not me – Marnie. And they're waiting.

I look up at my roommate. She's grinning again; it looks like she's chewing on something, transferring a small lump back and forth between her cheeks like a wad of gum.

"You never let me tell you what the sssssticky sssssstuff was for," Marnie says, and she opens her mouth.

I jerk awake at the sound of the phone ringing at my bedside. At first, I forget where I am, but then I notice the drawn curtains and closed door and I remember I had decided to lie down for a while, get some shut-eye.

I smack my lips – I always get this awful taste in my mouth after I take naps, like dusty old linen – and grab the phone off the nightstand. Look who it is, Landlord Jack at last.

"Hey Jessica," he says when I answer. "I'm sorry I haven't been responding to your texts or calls or anything, dropped my dang phone in the toilet on Friday and haven't been able to get in touch with anybody."

"No problem." I stretch. My body feels out of use.

"So you're still having bug problems, right? I've got a guy I can send over this afternoon—"

"No thanks," I tell him at once. "Taken care of."

Landlord Jack pauses.

"You sure? Your texts sounded pretty serious—"

"It's okay. Taken care of."

"Oh," he says, sounding relieved. "Good. I was afraid you had roaches, previous tenants had problems with those so you have no idea how relieved I am. But if you see any of them nasty things, just let me know and we'll get 'em gassed, lickety-split."

"Okay," I say, and hang up before he can add anything else. I drop the phone on the bed. I flex my hands. They are good hands and can do much more than spiny little limbs.

It is dark in here, dark and warm and nice. Easy to tell Jessica what to do. Whisper things into her pink human brain and watch as she does them. Hard to talk out of her mouth at first, speech is the hardest thing but after enough time we can do anything we want.

I am hungry. I think of the garbage in the kitchen and before I know it Jessica is up, stumbling out of her room, digging in the trash can for the things I crave: coffee grounds, fruit rinds, moldy bread crusts.

This is the one thing we cannot stop them from doing, eating when we are hungry, but that's all right. We find it very funny indeed.

Throughout the apartment, in the walls and under furniture and behind every shadow, I hear my brethren laughing: a low, long, whispery hiss.

16

FUIMUS NON SUMUS

It's always a shock. A surprise. No matter how much time you've had to prepare, whether it's cancer like a slow-acting poison in their veins or they suddenly drop dead of a heart attack, you're never ready for the utter reality of someone *being there* one moment and *gone* the next.

Everyone has their little niceties that, in truth, are more for their comfort than yours. The little greeting-card phrases like "everything happens for a reason" or "God works in mysterious ways." They don't explain anything. They don't tell you how you should act, or what you should feel, or what happens next. No one tells you what to do when your father dies. Even if they've been through it before, even if they've lost their own parent or child or beloved family pet, not one person will sit you down, look you in the eyes, and say "Here's what you do."

They don't tell you how to handle the dreams where he's still alive only to wake up hours later in a cold sweat. They don't warn you about the way every man on the street looks like him from behind, lurching your heart like a hot stone to the back of your throat until they turn their head to reveal no, you were wrong, it's not him after all.

No one tells you how hard it is to keep your secret, the vicious little ember deep in your stomach that knows you're glad he's dead, you're *glad* he's dead because it's over and he can't hurt you any more.

All the years of pretending it didn't happen, pushing the thoughts away, trying to douse that flame of hate in your belly... it's all been for nothing, and no one will tell you *why*.

They won't explain how the world starts to look like some bizarre silent film, all the pale people dressed in black weeping grandly at his funeral, how the only way you're not laughing like an insane person at this ridiculous farce of false grief is the way you've dug your nails into the palms of your hands until they draw blood.

All the people who thought they knew him, who had no idea of the monster that lurked beneath his skin, who touch your shoulder and mold their faces into masks of pity to console with words like "he'll always be with you." And how could they know? How could they know the ways he had already been with you, the slow creak of your bedroom door and the sliver of light that fell onto your bed, how it made your stomach greasy, your forehead peppered with tiny droplets of terror-sweat because you *knew* what was coming, you *knew* what would happen and yet there was no way to stop it?

Oh yes, he'll *always* be with you, that's something you know already.

No one tells you what comes next. What to do when you're an adult, alone in your bedroom at last, knowing the door will never open that way again because he's gone.

And no one tells you what to do when it *does*.

So you lay there, frozen, your skin clammy with the cold sweat of animal fear, waiting for what happens now because what you told yourself *never* happened, what you convinced yourself *never* had been, is back and it's at your door and it's *so* glad you haven't forgotten.

No one tells you what to do when your father dies, and no one tells you what to do when he comes back.

17

FOR EVERYTHING THERE IS A SEASON
(DANNY'S STORY)

Soft White Damn

"The snow doesn't give a soft white damn whom it touches."
—E. E. Cummings

It's been snowing forever. Every time it seems like it's about to let up, the sky clouds over with that flat white paper look and down it comes, more goddam snow.

I stopped shoveling the walk after the first two days. My dad was always real particular about his shoveling so I try to do the same but fuck, man. It was useless, I may as well have been that Greek guy with his boulder the way it piled up after I broke my damn back trying to clear a path. Told myself I'd do the neighborly thing and take care of it as soon as the thaw started but it hasn't started yet so it seemed like the best idea to just stay inside and stay warm. Make some soup and drink some whiskey.

And, after last night, drink more whiskey. Kind of a lot of whiskey.

You might think that was the problem, the whiskey, but no. I mean, I was drunk, but a good drunk, the nice easy drunk that makes your head buzz in the funniest way. I hadn't looked outside in a while; early on I'd pulled down one of the blinds to sneak a peek but saw only more fucking snow, the whole world was white and it was starting to piss me off so I let the blinds go with a little snapping sound that made me feel better for some reason. Like, yeah, take that, snow.

It was getting late but I wasn't really paying attention to the time. I only knew it was dark out because I hadn't moved from the couch to flip the lights when the gray-glow outside finally went down – you couldn't say that the sun set, not really because it wasn't out all day, it was hidden behind them damn thick snow clouds – and the living room was that weird kinda blue you get when your only source of light is a TV screen. I'd spent most of the day hopping from cable movie to cable movie, pretty bored but drunk enough by then that the sight of Goldie Hawn in *Overboard* wasn't too rough on the eyes. She's an annoying bitch in that one and she's got a mouth like an insane person but she's still pretty hot, so I'd settled in with a fresh glass of Jack (pants unzipped in case I felt frisky) and that was when the noises started.

Sort of quiet at first, so quiet I thought it was just snow or sleet hitting the windows. Then a little louder. Then, drunk or not I couldn't ignore it: tap-tap-tap-tap.

I was right, it was at the window for sure but no snow makes a noise like that. After I really heard it the first time I waited to see if it was a fluke. But after a second, again: tap-tap-tap-tap.

Not fast or nothing, and not random either. Real deliberate. Tap-tap-tap-TAP. Same sound it makes when you drum your fingers on a table if you're restless. Right on the windowpane of my porch window.

Someone was screwing with me, I was sure of it. Maybe pissed I hadn't shoveled the walk yet. Out there, tapping on my window in the middle of a blizzard just to hock me off.

I waited another minute. I didn't turn down *Overboard* in case they were listening close – didn't want them to know I knew they were out there, I was gonna catch them off guard, see – and when I heard tap-tap-tap I snapped down one of the blinds, ready to make mean eyes at some punk kid or nosy neighbor.

Nothing out there, though.

Weird, too, because the tapping, it was on the glass right there, right behind those blinds.

I half-watched the movie for about 10 minutes, waiting for the tapping to start up again, but it didn't. Pretty soon I'd drained half the glass of Jack and I was feeling okay again, a little jumpy I guess but it hadn't really scared me, not yet.

It was just getting to the part where Goldie really gives it to that snooty teacher when I heard something else. It started quiet again, getting a little louder every minute until I couldn't write off the noise on the storm. This time, I did mute the movie, and almost immediately wished I hadn't.

It was this low voice – couldn't tell if it was a man or a woman but it was low – and it was talking. Only that's not right because it wasn't really saying anything, it wasn't saying words, just sort of gibbering, a constant babble of sounds and wheezy grunts that meant nothing.

And it wasn't like another language or anything either. Like, you know when you hear another language, and even though you can't understand them you know they're saying *something?* Maybe it's the way they say it, I dunno, but this was different.

My dad had a stroke when I was a kid. We were out shopping for a gift for my mom's birthday and I asked him if he wanted to look at cards and when he opened his mouth he started talking, but it wasn't words, it was just garbled stuff, and he *knew* he wasn't saying the right thing but he couldn't fix it. I hadn't thought of that in years but the sounds outside? They were like that. That's the closest I can get.

Whatever it was heard me turn down the volume and got louder, gibbering like my dad that day in April, and for a horrible second I actually thought it *was* my dad's voice, but he's been dead a long time so there was no way, and it felt like as soon as I let go of that memory and that thought the gibbering sounded less like him until I was sure no, it wasn't my dead dad out there on the porch in the snowstorm. I was drunk, like I said, and for a minute I felt kinda sad about that.

My head, it felt kinda funny too. Like I'd been watching TV in the dark too long. The buzzing that was nice earlier sounded more like hornets than bumblebees now. I finished the glass of whiskey, slammed it on the table, and looked through the blinds again.

Nothing out there. Snowing, still, harder than ever. But nothing on the porch. And right away, the gibbering stopped.

I don't know why I looked like that. I should've been more careful, I didn't know what could be out there, if it was a homeless guy or whatever trying to find a warm place to sleep in the storm but a part of me also knew it wasn't a homeless guy and that I should've been more careful when I looked because homeless guys don't sound like your dead dad no matter how drunk you are.

It was okay, though, because nothing was on the porch. But I didn't unmute *Overboard* and I was pretty quick to get some more whiskey.

A few minutes went by – probably the same as before, if I really think about it – and now I heard something running, full-on *running* back and forth across the porch, something with big heavy footsteps and an awful lot of speed.

Every third run or so I'd hear it throw itself against the wooden banisters at either end of the porch. The wood would groan and whatever it was would let out some weird chuffing sound, not like it had knocked the wind out of itself, more like it was laughing.

I didn't know what to do, I was too scared to look now and really wishing I hadn't had so much to drink (or maybe that I'd had much, much more) but after the latest slam against the banister I thought I heard wood splinter and without thinking I yelled, "Hey, STOP!"

It did. It got real quiet. The phone was in the kitchen, I should've called the cops but it didn't even cross my mind because then:

"Dannydannydannydanny."

It was the same babbling voice from before, and it made my name sound like gibberish, like my name didn't fit right in its mouth.

"Dannydannydannydanny." It wasn't running anymore, it sounded like it was shifting from foot to foot, back and forth back and forth, fast like when a kid gets hyper or has to pee. It was right outside the front door.

"Dannydannydannydanny are you *sorry* Dannydannydanny?" it said, and my stomach suddenly felt like it was full of cold mud. "Are you *sorry* Dannydannydanny you're sorry aren't you Dannydannydanny? Oh Dannydannydannydanny your daddy knows, oh yes Dannydannydanny your daddy's here..."

It sounded like my dad again, yeah, but not really, the way a funhouse mirror looks like you but not really.

"Come outside Dannydannydanny," it said, "daddy's here, daddy's back, Dannydannydanny, open the door, you forgot to shovel the walk Dannydannydanny, daddy's awful mad at you..."

I looked down and I was standing at the door, reaching for the knob. I didn't remember even getting off the couch, or setting my drink down, or zipping my pants back up.

"I didn't forget to shovel," I told it, stepping slowly away from the door. "I'm gonna do it when it stops snowing."

"Oh Dannydannydanny," it said, "don't you know it's never going to stop? Oh, aren't you *sorry*, Dannydannydannydanny, you're going to be *so* sorry if you don't get out here and see your dad-deeeeeee..."

"My dad's not out there." I said this more to me than to whatever was on the porch. It felt good, like I was getting a handle on something, so I said it again. "My dad's not out there, it's the middle of a damn snowstorm and he's been dead 15 years and I don't know what you are but you're not my dad."

The gibbering started again. It stopped saying my name and went back to running back and forth across the porch like it was throwing a tantrum.

I dunno why it latched onto my dad. Maybe because he was the first thing I thought of? Maybe because I hadn't thought about him in a long time? Like I said, I dunno, but I listened to it barreling across my porch, babbling sometimes in my dad's voice, sometimes in the same low voice I heard first, sometimes something else entirely.

It ran back and forth on the porch for almost four hours. I never unmuted the TV, just stared at the blinds covering the windows to the porch and finished the bottle of Jack.

Finally, the sun came up. I mean, not really, the sky got ivory white and the sun was behind the clouds somewhere but the important part is it got light out and the thing stopped. I was pretty wasted by then but I waited another half hour, waited to be sure it was gone and that morning had really made it go.

Remember how I said more whiskey? Kind of a lot of whiskey? Well, I meant it, I'm gonna need a lot more to get through this. Because well, I checked the weather report today, and another winter storm is coming through tonight. Up to six more inches by tomorrow morning. And the thing is, I don't know if I'll make it to tomorrow morning. That thing is gonna come back, it just is, and this time I don't know what it's gonna say but what I do know is that the first time it came, I almost opened the goddamn door for it.

The other thing, the other reason I started drinking as soon as I woke up this afternoon, is what I saw before I finally passed out after my all-nighter with the whatever outside. What I saw when I finally did open the door and look at the porch.

The snow is deep, maybe up to my shins if I really get out there and wade in it, but it's not so deep on the porch. Since it's covered, you know. But there's enough to leave tracks.

And the damndest thing is – there are tracks. But only hands.

No footprints. None at all. Just a hundred handprints, all over my snow-dusted porch, clear as day.

Sorry if this doesn't make much sense. I'm drunk and it doesn't make much sense to me either. But it's gonna be dark soon and all I can think about is what's coming back, what speaks in my dad's voice, what walks on its hands in the snow in the night.

And you know what?

I *am* sorry.

———

Sure to Follow

"No matter how long the winter, spring is sure to follow."
—Ancient Proverb

It took three days. Three god damn days for the snow to stop but when it did, I packed up my things and got gone in a hurry. I didn't even shovel the walk before I left. Fuck it.

I mean, it wasn't like I had to give notice or anything. Dad's money makes life pretty easy and I don't need much. Besides, I've got places all over. Feels good to shake the dust off – or in this case, the snow – and stay somewhere else for a while. Especially, you know, after what happened.

I decided to head to New Orleans. The Big Easy. There's no place like Bourbon Street in the world, I tell you, so full of life and booze and half-coherent women. My favorite things. Main problem is the rain. There's a reason they don't bury their dead in Louisiana, stick 'em in big concrete boxes above ground instead. But rain isn't snow and I can survive. I'm good like that.

I had a place on the outskirts of town. Close enough I could go into the city and have some fun but far enough from the constant buzz of

NOLA activity that I wouldn't be bothered. I mean, who can listen to jazz that often without going crazy? Jazz is fine and all but there's a limit.

Was okay for a while. Started to suspect that maybe I'd even imagined the whole thing, tricked myself into thinking there had been something on the porch by way of whiskey and boredom. I mean, I'd been cooped up for days. What do they call that – cabin fever, right?

Yeah. It was probably that, right?

Then came the rain.

It started as a drizzle. I was heading home from the bar after a fairly successful night and suddenly it was spitting little droplets onto my windshield, the annoying kind that you barely need wipers for but if you don't use them you can't really see and it honestly pissed me off, this small thing that shouldn't have mattered but did somehow. It was a black smudge on what had been a pretty good time and... I guess... it reminded me of the snow.

When I got home I made sure to latch all the fancy new locks I'd bought for my doors. No use taking chances. By then, it was pouring.

I'd barely fixed myself a glass of Jack – old habits die hard – when I heard the knock.

I froze. It couldn't be.

Just like before, I waited. Hoping to God or Jesus or all the angels in heaven that I hadn't heard what I knew I had. Enough time passed, rain pounding steady on the roof, that for a brief blessed moment I actually thought that yeah, I'd heard something, but it was just the storm and nothing else.

Again: a knock. Then another.

I knew by now not to look outside. Not to check the porch. Last time, that seemed to let it in my head somehow. Let it get me off the couch and almost open the door.

Then:

"Mister?"

It was a little voice, a kid's voice. He sounded alright, sorta familiar, barely audible over the rain. Maybe it was a neighbor? Maybe he sounded like someone I'd heard on TV? All possibilities, sure, most important though he sounded alright.

But I still couldn't make myself look out there.

"Yeah?" I called, inching towards the door. "Who is it?" Like I said, I'm on the outskirts of town. I pay attention real close to my neighbors. I didn't remember seeing a kid.

"Mister, let me in," the kid said, his voice shaking like it does when you're trying not to cry but pretty close to failing. "I was with my dad and he left me in the car and I don't know where he is. It's been real long, I'm getting so worried..."

For a second, my heart went out to the kid. It really did. My dad did something like that to me too, once. When I was real little.

Then I realized.

"How long's he been gone?" I asked, and my voice wasn't shaking, but I sorta was.

"Almost two hours," the kid said miserably. "He parked outside of some house, I don't know who lives there, he told me to be a good boy and wait."

Of course he did. I remembered that much. But, like my dad, I hadn't thought about it in a long time.

Suddenly, wildly, the doorknob began to rattle.

"Please let me in," the kid pleaded. "It's cold and wet out here, I'm soaked and I don't know where my dad is."

"You didn't wait," I said, the glass of Jack sweating in the hot palm of my hand. "You got out and that's real bad, kid, he told you to be a good boy and wait."

A long, tense pause while the doorknob kept rattling.

"I s'pose," the kid said, sorta thoughtfully, "Daddy might be awful mad if he finds out I didn't stay in the car, huh?"

"Yeah." I exhaled, took a big swig of whiskey, swallowed. It was like swallowing cold metal. "He was."

The doorknob stopped moving.

I suddenly knew why the kid had sounded familiar. It wasn't a neighbor. It wasn't someone I'd heard on TV.

It was me.

"Dan-eeeeee," he said slowly, drawing the last sound out long and low. "Dan-eeeeee. Eeeeee. Eeeeee."

I told you my dad was real particular about things, like shoveling the walk when it snowed. He was also real particular about rules. And obeying them.

"We waited as long as we could," I said, like talking to this Other-Me outside the door was normal, fine, not batshit crazy. "We waited, kid, I know that, but it was such a long time."

"Dad-eeeeee got mad, didn't he Dan-eeeeee?" It was still my voice, the voice of me when I was eight and my dad left me in the car, and that was somehow worse. The funhouse-mirror version in the snow had been better because I could tell myself there was something wrong, something bad, but this just sounded like... me.

"Yeah, he sure did," I said. "But he told us, you know, he told us to be good and what did we do? Got right out of the car and started snooping like spoiled little shits." Another swig. "We deserved what we got."

"Are you sorry, Dan-eeeeee?" he said. "Are you sorry for what you did Dan-eeeeee, eeeeee, eeeeee? You didn't get what's coming to you, aren't you sorry?"

I remembered the whooping I got when we got home that night. I had gotten what was coming, all right.

Outside, the rain poured.

"No, we got punished." I had already sorta resigned to myself that this was happening, there was no getting away from it, so I sat down on the couch closest to the door and swallowed half the glass. "Don't you remember? We got it good. Could barely sit down for a week."

He'd used the belt that time. The part with the buckle.

"Dan-eeeeeee. Eeeeeee. Eeeeeee." Slow, deliberate slaps against the door, like palms smacking on wood. "Let me in. Let me in. Let me in."

I exhaled through my nose. The world was starting to dim around the edges but I tried to ground myself. Took another sip, hoping it would warm my insides – which had become cold, sick.

I didn't answer.

"Dan-eeeeeee. Eeeeeee. Eeeeeee. If you don't let me in, he'll get me. He'll get us."

I didn't answer.

"Aren't you sorr-EEEEEEEEEEEEEEEEEEEEEEEE!" it shrieked, and then it was like there were a thousand hands all at once, slapping the wood, the frame, the windows –

Oh god. The windows.

I'd thought to put locks on the doors but not the god damn windows.

I dropped the glass, grabbed my car keys and went for the back like a bat out of hell. I'd left something important in the basement but it didn't matter, nothing mattered except getting away from that fucking thing.

The screen door stuck at first when I tried to open it. Nearly went barreling through the metal mesh. The stupid handle caught, it catches sometimes and it caught then, and behind me I heard one of the front windows open so hard the glass shattered.

I slammed against the door with my shoulder and the handle caught again, then broke. I fell through, started to run.

My car was parked in a shed behind the house. It's more private that way.

I like my privacy. Just like my dad.

With unsteady hands I wrenched the shed doors open, boots slipping in the mud. I was already drenched.

I made my way to the car when I heard it: quick, thick squelching sounds.

Something was behind me, and it was moving fast.

I threw myself into the car and jabbed the keys blindly into the ignition. Someone must've been looking out for me because I got it the first time, lurched the car into gear, and drove straight through the back wall of the shed.

Splintered wood went flying everywhere. The car fishtailed, its tires finding little traction in the mud, but soon I was off the grass and on the little gravel road that wound around my property. It led, eventually, to the highway, and that's how I got to the hotel where I'll be staying for a while.

I don't know who's listening. I don't know who cares. But if you are, if you do, do you need me to tell you that when I went back – in the daylight, of course – the front of my house was covered in filthy, muddy handprints?

Of course not.

What I didn't expect, I guess, is for them to be so low to the ground. Like it couldn't reach too high. Like a kid couldn't.

I don't know where I'm going next. It comes in the snow, it comes in the rain. It keeps... coming... back.

But like I said, I've got places all over. And what it doesn't know about me is how well I can survive. I survived my dad, you know? I can survive this.

And if I don't, I guess I'll get what's coming to me.

Every Leaf is a Flower

"Autumn is a second spring when every leaf is a flower."
—*Albert Camus*

I managed to make it a few more months.

Got to a new place, set up shop, went back to New Orleans for just a day trip to clear out my business in the basement. No one had messed with it, that was good, that was why I picked such a remote place in the first place. Me and my dad, we liked our privacy. You probably know that by now.

I went north this time, followed the ocean along the east and tried to find somewhere safe, somewhere dry. Somewhere that no one could leave handprints.

That's what was following me, right? The handprints? The voice? Worse, what was *attached* to those handprints?

It was always different, but it was always the same. My father, something else, my childhood, something else. Shifting, changing, unpredictable and terrifying. I wanted to tell someone about it but who was there to tell? Ma was in the ground five years now, my dad a lot longer than that. What they don't tell you about growing up is how alone you end up feeling.

I hunkered down in my place in the north. Waited. Because I knew it was coming. It had to be coming, right? The quiet was starting to get to me, it was worse somehow that I knew it was coming and knew it wouldn't stop but didn't know when or how.

It got so goddam close last time, you know? That Other Me, the thing that sounded like myself as a kid, like myself at age eight when my dad had left me in the car parked outside some strange house for hours. Hadn't thought about that in a real long time, not until Other Me jogged some memories.

I started to think about it, though. While I waited. About how it took so long for my dad to come back, he'd told me to wait but I couldn't, I had to pee and I was worried so I figured getting out of the car for just a minute wouldn't hurt. Right? I mean, sure my dad was strict, but how could you expect a little kid to wait that long by himself?

After a while, summer faded into fall and it still hadn't shown up. Was it because we had a mild season? No snow, no rain, no crazy weather to bring it on? I hoped so. But when I started seeing that thin sheen of frost on my porch early in the morning, I decided it might be best to fix my sleep schedule. Like, no more late-night drinks, keep the whiskey to the daytime and fall into bed by 6pm, before nightfall. My dad did that, you know, after he got off the third shift for a few years. He said it did him good.

Main thing is, I didn't want to hear what could be outside. It only came at night and I was so tired of waiting, you know? I thought it might be best to just shut myself off during the times it could come. Because either it couldn't (or wouldn't) get inside without my help, or if it did, maybe I'd just go peacefully. In my sleep. That was a nice thought.

Then, once I started getting more sleep, I didn't just think about that night outside the strange house. I started to dream about it.

In the dreams, I'm little again — or maybe I'm not? I feel short but when I look at my hands they're man's hands, leathery and tough. Maybe they're my dad's hands. I don't know.

I use these hands to knock on the door. I have that tight, tense sensation in my bladder, the pinching need to pee. I cross my legs back and forth, hoping someone will come to the door but they never do. So I go to a window.

When I look inside, I see my dad. He's with a woman. It's not my mom.

He sees me, too. And he's real mad.

He yells, "DANNY!"

Then I wake up.

The same dream, over and over. The same way every time: in the car, have to pee, knock on the door, go to the window, dad with the woman. "DANNY!"

And see, here's the weird thing. I only have this dream in the daytime. Never had it at night.

Well, I guess maybe *that's* not the weirdest thing.

No, no handprints yet or anything. Nothing like that. But since the leaves have started to change, since they've gotten all colorful, red and orange and yellow, they've started showing up in my house.

First, they were on the porch. But that's pretty normal, right? Gust of wind blows 'em up there, no cause for concern. But then one day you wake up just after dawn, like usual, happy to see the sun coming up over the horizon, and you see a trail of them from your front door to the dining room. And they're pretty at first, see, they're those brilliant fall shades but they still have enough springy life in them to stay in one piece. At first, you sort of like them.

Then, as the season goes on, as you have the same dream over and over again about your dad and the woman and your big man hands, they start to die. They get crunchy and crumbly and you start to find them everywhere. Trailing through the house. Stuffed in your dresser drawers. Folded into quarters and stuck neatly between the bills in your wallet.

It's deliberate. It's a message. It's what it does when it can't leave handprints.

One morning you wake up coughing, sputtering, tongue drier than you can ever remember. You spit and spit and wouldn't you know, you're spitting out a mouthful of brittle autumn leaves.

Something has come into your house in the middle of the night and stuffed your fucking mouth with leaves.

God only knows what would've happened if you'd been awake when it came. Then, you wonder — is it really your dad you're hearing in the dreams? Is it really your dad yelling your name, or is it something... else? Something crouched by your bed as it parts your lips and begins shoving dead leaves inside?

And this, you know, this is what makes you realize you can't get away from it. You can't keep running. You could try, of course, you could keep sleeping through its cycle or moving with the weather or whatever, but one day you'll choke to death on whatever else it's decided to shove in your mouth and maybe next time it won't be as harmless as leaves.

So you — I — pack up and go to the last place you saw your dad alive. The last place you have really good, happy memories.

And you leave the leaves behind.

———

The Earth, the Air, and You

"Like a welcome summer rain, humor may suddenly cleanse and cool the earth, the air and you."
—Langston Hughes

I went back to Arizona. To my dad's old place. Like I said, I've got places all over, but most of them are mine. This one was my dad's. This one was my favorite.

It took a few days to get my sleep schedule back on track. To get ready. Because after the snow, the mud, the leaves — I knew there was no escaping it. Best I could do was go back to the only place I considered home.

My dad bought the place, a modest little bungalow plopped out in the middle of the desert — remote, private, you bet — after Ma filed for divorce. She found out what he'd been up to and finally found herself a spine. I don't think my dad much cared, to be honest. He didn't fight her, didn't screw her out of what she asked for, either. Gave her a fair amount of money and jetted down to sunny Arizona. Almost like he was relieved.

I spent my teenage years bouncing back and forth between Ma's place and my dad's. It wasn't so bad. When I wasn't in school, my dad let me drink with him. He'd be in his armchair, the same bulky armchair that sits in my living room now like a dozing brown bear. "Nothin' wrong with a little Jack Daniels between men," he'd say. What he didn't say was that even though I saw what he was doing in that strange house, I never told Ma, even though he belted me good when we got home that night. I think that made him respect me.

I didn't ask questions, either, when he left for long periods of time. My dad had always been private and even though I was older I had no doubt I'd get the belt again if I went snooping. When he got drunk, he could get mean, and sometimes he'd come back stinking plastered, looking for a chore to keep him busy. No snow in Arizona, no walk to shovel, so every now and then I'd hear him out in the backyard digging. He was the kind of man who had to keep his hands busy. Couldn't fault him for that, I guess.

Once I was back to normal, feeling like maybe I could stay up pretty late, I bought myself a bottle of Jack and settled in the living room. Sank into my dad's old armchair. I turned on the television and began flipping channels. Sadly enough, I couldn't find "Overboard" on anywhere.

I drank my whiskey. Kind of a lot of whiskey.

And sure enough, after about an hour, it started.

Tap-tap-tap-tap.

I switched off the television. Finished my drink. Poured another one.

"I hear you out there," I called. "Didn't take you too long this time, did it?"

Tap-tap-tap-tap.

"What's it gonna be, huh?" I demanded. Jack had made me brave, braver than before, so I slammed another swig back and felt the warmth spread through my stomach. "Are you my dad? Are you me? Gonna yell at me for not shoveling the walk? Ha! No snow out there, asshole, and no rain neither. We don't get any rain in these parts, not that often. Just sand and sun."

Tap-tap-tap-tap. On one window, the one on the porch. Then I heard it in the kitchen, too. And towards the back of the house, in the mudroom. Tapping on all the windows. There were more this time.

And when it spoke, that's when I knew I'd made a mistake — that I'd missed the whole goddam point. That I was absolutely, utterly fucked.

Not my dad. Not me. Not even the wordless babbling. Worse. Much, much worse.

"Danny, oh Danny, Danny," it said in a sweet, feminine voice. A voice I didn't really recognize but also sort of did. "Danny, oh Danny, we're out here, Danny. We're here. You thought we couldn't find you, but we did."

No.

No.

There was no way.

I'd made sure, I'd been so careful.

"Danny, oh Danny, Danny," it crooned again, and there was nothing wrong with the voice really, just sounded like a normal lady, someone I might meet on one of my nights out, someone I almost certainly did. "Danny, oh Danny, you thought we couldn't get to you but we did. We're here, come outside, say hello, oh Danny, don't you like us anymore? You liked us so much, too much, didn't you?"

I felt like my mouth had been stuffed full of leaves again. My stomach wasn't warm anymore, it lurched like I'd swallowed a gallon of cold, thick mud.

"Danny, oh Danny, you just did what your daddy taught you. We're not angry, Danny, we're not mad, those were our friends we sent before, we couldn't get to you first so we sent them along and they were the old ones, they were the angry ones, but we're fresh and new and we want to know why you left us, Danny."

I gripped the glass of whiskey so tight I thought it might shatter.

"You can't be out there," I said when I could move my tongue again. "None of you, I made sure you couldn't walk, I made sure—"

They shouldn't have been able to get out of the basement. I learned that, I learned from my dad, if you let them stay mobile they can almost get away, that lady in the house that night *almost* got away because I distracted him at the window, she bolted but my dad was faster and he took her down but I'm not that fast so it was always just easier to cut off their feet.

"Danny, oh Danny, we figured it out, we're smart girls, Danny, did you know if you try hard enough you can walk on your hands?" It sounded so nice, like it wasn't mad at all, not like the others, but oh god I wasn't sure it was telling the truth. "It took us longer, the lot of us, oh Danny it took us a while to try hard enough but we did, we can do it now, just like our friends. Our angry friends. Oh Danny, did you know when you're angry you try much harder?"

Yeah, that I knew. When you think your dad is the best guy in the world but really he's just a bully, he thinks he's so much better than you and hits you with the buckle end of his belt for just being a kid when it was *him* who was being bad, *him* who was in there strangling some woman who probably was gonna tell Ma about what they'd been up to. When he punishes you again and again for things you didn't mean to do, like forgetting to shovel the walk. For getting mud on the porch. For not getting all the leaves in the yard bagged just right. Yeah, you get angry. And you try much harder. To be better than him.

"I think he only did the one," I mused, finally lifting the glass to my lips with a trembling hand. "I think it was just the one, if I had to guess."

"Oh Danny," it said, and it sounded aroused, like it was getting hot or something. "Danny, *oh* Danny, you did *so* much more, didn't you?"

Tap-tap-tap-tap. At all the windows. How were they tapping? If they walked on their hands, how were they tapping, oh god as if any of this made any sense at all...

How many of them were out there? Some of them? Dear god, *all* of them?

"You left me in the basement, Danny," it said, sad now, pouty, a girlfriend who's not getting her way. "You came back, oh Danny, yes you did, but I was so smelly by then, and when you left I hadn't even gone yet, I was still there, still *alive*, and my feet, oh Danny why did you cut off my feet? It hurt, Danny, oh Danny you hurt me so! You hurt *us* so!"

Unbelievably, I heard more tapping — but this tapping was rain. It was fucking raining. Again.

"You were all so easy," I said, wiping a thin sheen of sweat from my upper lip with the back of my hand. "Buy you a few drinks, bring you home, knock you out. Maybe if it hadn't been so easy—"

"Oh Danny, don't *lie*, don't be a little *liar*, you did it to show your daddy, didn't you? And you showed your daddy, oh Danny, we know that now, we know what you did, your daddy is awful mad at you for what you did..."

The rain fell harder, harder, like a fucking monsoon. I couldn't hear the tapping on the windows anymore but I knew they were out there, all of them, because why not all of them?

On the porch, something began running back and forth. Back and forth. I thought I heard a little kid laugh but couldn't be sure.

I felt like I was losing my mind, thoughts were slippery and escaping from me, *they were all out there.*

"Are you sitting in his chair, Danny?" it said, louder now to be heard over the downpour. "Oh Danny, are you sitting in the chair where you did it? He told us about it, Danny, he's awful mad at you, oh Danny, oh Danny..."

"I had to wait 'till I got big enough," I murmured. "Strong enough. I had to do it with my own hands, just like he did."

"Danny, oh Danny, you wrapped your big strong hands around his neck and you showed your daddy, didn't you? 15 years ago, oh Danny, oh *yes* Danny, that's what you did, we know what you did, your daddy wants you to get what's coming to you and now it's raining and now we're done talking and now we're coming inside and now you're going to be *so sorry.*"

The front door burst open. I heard windows, windows in other rooms, all the windows, shattering. And there they were.

The blonde I'd brought home in Texas. The redhead with the huge tits I scored in Minnesota. The mousy little brunette I'd settled for in New

Orleans, the one I'd left in the basement when the whatever on the porch came through the window.

Scores of them. All of them. Had there really been that many? Crawling through the broken glass, unaware of the way their rotting skin was being shredded to ribbons. A few were dragging themselves forward by their elbows, trailing bloody stumps where their feet had once been.

Most, though, were walking on their hands. And goddam were they fast. They must've been angrier than they let on.

I dropped my drink and scrambled to the back of the house, to the kitchen where the phone was. I'd tried to handle this myself and it was out of my hands, I had to get help, I had to get someone out here to *help,* oh god why had I moved to this godforsaken place in the middle of nowhere?

Outside, the rain poured, buckets of it.

When I got to the kitchen, I fumbled with the phone on the cradle, nearly dropping it in my panic, and looked behind me.

They had me surrounded. My house stunk of decaying flesh. Some of the older ones, their jaws hung crookedly from their skulls. But they were just... waiting.

The ones on their elbows were crouched, tense, ready to pounce. The ones on their hands swayed with an eerie expert balance.

Slowly, unaware if they could see me now that I was still — many of them had no eyes, after all, just gaping dark holes in their heads — I punched nine-one-one. I brought the phone to my ear. As the dead women watched, I told the operator that I was being attacked and needed help. They said help was on the way. I wondered if it would be soon enough and replaced the phone on the hook.

The brunette (the mousy one from New Orleans) shifted back and forth, back and forth on her hands, like an excited little kid.

"Danny, oh Danny, you're going to be so sorry!" she squealed through decaying lips. I wasn't even sure how she could make sounds with those lips.

A tittering spread through the crowd, a slurpy sort of giggling that almost couldn't be heard over the heavy rain.

"Danny, Danny, Danny," the women said in droning unison. "Danny, Danny, Danny."

I put my hands over my ears.

"Stop! Leave me alone!" I screamed. "You were stupid sluts, you were just like the one my dad did, you got what was coming to you!"

"Oh Danny," the brunette cried as the rest of them kept saying my name. "Oh Danny, you showed your daddy, you showed *us*, and now you're going to be so sorry, now you're going to see your daddy again! You'll be like us, you'll get what's coming to you, yes you will, oh Danny!"

They said my name, over and over. It began to sound like a song.

I rocked back and forth, shouting nonsense at them, trying to drown out the rain and the chorus of dead women crooning my name. I backed up against the sink, hands clamped over my ears. I don't know how long I was like that but they got louder, louder, *louder* until —

"Ha!" I cried out, triumphant, and opened my eyes to look at the 37 rotting bodies that filled the house where I'd murdered my father. "You hear that, you dumb bitches, that's the police! They're coming, they're gonna save me!" Indeed, the women had stopped singing, and through the rain I heard the distinctive wail of a cop car's siren.

But they were smiling.

"Oh Danny," sighed the brunette from New Orleans, "look in the backyard."

My blood ran cold.

No. There was no way.

I turned and looked out the window that oversaw the backyard. The backyard of dry, packed desert dirt. The backyard where my dad used to dig and the backyard where I eventually did my own digging, too.

He liked Arizona because it was dry. Because it never rained. But tonight, oh how it had rained. And it turns out, I was wrong. He'd done more than one.

Just like me.

In the backyard, the tightly-packed desert dirt was mostly gone — under the downpour it had become a thin murky soup. In it floated swollen, bloated carcasses. Bones stripped of flesh. A few heads that still had wispy hair on them even as the skull gleamed beneath it.

I knew they weren't all mine, not that many bones, but that didn't much matter. The siren was louder now, right outside. It didn't take long for me to put the pieces together.

They would see the bodies. They would check my other places. They would find out what I'd done with my big, strong hands. All because I couldn't wait in the car.

I turned back to the living room and was unsurprised to find it empty. No rotting women. Those were in the backyard. The interior of my house suddenly began to flash blue, red, blue, red. And I began to laugh.

What is it they say about the sins of the father? It doesn't matter. Because I lied.

I'm *not* sorry.

18

BEST WISHES, IRENE MILLER

She studied her face in the mirror. Turned her chin this way, then that, unhappy with what the harsh makeup lights illuminated. Pinched her cheeks, hoping to give them some flush. Irene wasn't feeling it today, the razzle-dazzle quality she knew she'd need if she was going to hold her own onstage. As if she had a choice.

The Tipton Sisters were performing. It was bullshit, having to compete with circus freaks for the audience's already brief attention. She was Irene Miller, for God's sake — she'd performed with Buster Keaton, and yet she was lowered to sharing the bill with Siamese Twins.

Irene didn't like that, the meanness in her heart. Lily and Rose were sweet girls. It wasn't their fault their mother had a drinking problem and forced their oddness in the spotlight to afford the next bottle of hooch. She didn't want to be like the others, the jugglers and the magicians and the clowns dressed up in gay mockery of bums that shuffled the streets. They were full of meanness, leathery-tough and quick to anger when they thought their stardom was being taken from them. Irene didn't want to feel the way they did and yet she couldn't help it; she got all panicky in her chest when she thought about a playbill without her name.

There were rumblings that the Big Men Upstairs wanted to bring on a colored act. The clowns protested that they could double their own routine, do one in blackface and one in full circus makeup, but the Big Men Upstairs didn't seem to be buying it. "Not authentic," they said, and the troop got a little more uneasy day by day. Someone was likely to be booted from the lineup, and soon.

Irene licked her thumb, smoothing a stray hair that had escaped her perfectly-curled style.

Behind her, at her own vanity, Florence was applying lipstick.

"Did you hear about Jennie Del Vecchio?" she asked, making eye contact with Irene's reflection in the mirror.

Irene shook her head. The stray hair popped up again and she sighed.

"What about Jennie Del Vecchio?" she responded, not really caring all that much. Gossip made its way around the troop like disease in a camp of sick soldiers.

"Coppers picked her up last night. Caught her in an alley with her skirt hiked up. She was with a john."

Irene frowned. She turned in her seat to look at Florence but Florence didn't turn around and she ended up staring at the back of her head.

"She's only been out a few weeks," Irene said in disbelief. "Didn't she leave here with pay? I thought she'd been saving."

Florence shrugged.

"Who knows. Maybe she blew through it. Everyone knows she drinks like a fish anyway." There it was again, that meanness. Irene hated it.

"She's young, though," Irene murmured to Florence's fat blonde curls of hair.

"Not young enough. Thirteen and ugly to boot. Soon as she started the Curse she got all..." Florence paused, looking for the right word. "...knobby. Not pretty anymore like when she was a baby. Can't call a knobby thirteen-year-old Baby Jennie."

Irene considered this. She thought it was very rude that Florence wouldn't turn around and look at her.

"But... johns? So soon?"

"Just like my mama told me," Florence said breezily, smacking her rosy lips together to set the lipstick. "'A woman's only as good as what she's got between her legs.'" She made eye contact with Irene in the mirror again and added, noting her baffled expression, "Not you and me, a'course. We're better than that, we're *stars*."

Irene turned back towards her own vanity. She suddenly felt her reflection looked very old. She pinched her cheeks again.

"You danced with Buster Keaton," Florence added in what was probably supposed to be a helpful tone.

Outside the tent, there was a wild whoop of laughter. Men, and drunk from the sound of it. Irene hoped they wouldn't come in; she didn't have the patience to smile and fend them off this particular evening.

"You finish your cabinet cards?" Florence was rubbing big pink circles of rouge on her cheeks. Irene considered asking her for some, then decided against it. She didn't want be in debt to Florence for anything. She looked sweet but she could be as ugly to deal with as a rattlesnake sometimes.

"I still got about a hundred to do. I ran out of ink so I'm doing them in pencil. It doesn't look so good but it'll do for now." Irene cast a glance at the wooden crate of pale brown photographs near her feet. A hundred stacked versions of her own face stared back at her, waiting to be flourished with her signature. In pencil, like an amateur. Out of rouge and out of ink until the next pay came in.

One of the clowns stuck his head through the flaps of their tent. His face was painted garishly, yet sloppily, as though he'd done it in a hurry. He looked more like something out of a nightmare than a performer meant to make children laugh.

He left again without a word. Irene assumed he was looking for one of the singers, who usually had the white powder that fueled their lunatic onstage scampering.

"You want some rouge?" Florence asked her, finally turning around. "You're sort of pale."

Irene stared at her own face in the mirror. God, how old she looked. The cabinet cards at her feet seemed to mock her with their uneven brown printing: Little Irene. What a joke. She felt no more 'little' than Jennie Del Vecchio, who could no longer call herself 'Baby Jennie' and was laying on her back in dirty alleyways just a few weeks after being fired from the troop.

"Just a bit," she said, defeated. Florence got up from her vanity and set the tin down delicately in front of Irene.

"Say, isn't your birthday coming up soon?" Florence seemed to sense her uneasiness; she fussed over Irene's hair, putting stray strands in their place, trying to make her perfect. "How old will you be, Irene?"

Irene sighed. She needed to start on the cabinet cards. She picked up her pencil, took a handful of the cardboard-mounted photographs, and began the laborious process of signing her name. 'Best Wishes, Irene Miller.' She couldn't bring herself to add the 'Little' this time.

"Nine," she said, and kept signing.

19

ONCE BITTEN

This is what you asked for.

Right?

Something to keep you awake at night? Something to make your skin crawl and set your teeth on edge?

Take a deep breath.

You can read as many articles from *Jezebel* and *Cosmo* that say you don't have to sleep your way to the top, not anymore, but keep in mind those women have jobs writing for women's magazines and *their* top is already within reach; they're not in a field dominated by men who keep an eye out for every sweet young thing on their way through the door. They haven't spent years kissing ass, flashing smiles, and working 80-hour weeks only to watch lawyers still wet behind the ears get promotions over them. They're not me.

So I decided to change tactics.

About a month ago I noticed one of the senior partners giving me the eye during the boardroom meetings. This guy was a shark, the kind of lawyer who can make you weak in the knees and warm in the crotch at the same time. You knew he was a sleaze but he was a sleaze you'd ride until his eyes rolled back.

And power. He had *power*. He could give me the promotion I'd been killing myself for and he'd probably just want to tie me to the bed while we fucked. I could do that.

Other people jabbered through the meeting but his eyes were on me, just me. Maybe it was the red lipstick I'd worn that day or the dab of perfume behind my neck. Either way I returned his looks, subtly but with purpose, running my tongue over my teeth when I knew he could see.

He liked that, I could see it in the way his salt-and-pepper eyebrows dipped low over his dark eyes. He had a face like a wolf's, sharp and lean. He looked like a man who took what he wanted, and I wanted him to want me.

I knew what to do. Run into him in the elevator when I'd unbuttoned my top a little too low. Drop pencils near his desk and bend over, slowly, to retrieve them. Eye contact, girls, lots and lots of eye contact. It's really not that hard.

Before the week was over I was in his bedroom, our naked bodies moving together, teeth nipping at my salty skin. He liked to bite, I found that out soon enough. Our first time together he grasped my lower lip between his teeth, sucking hard, and then suddenly I felt him break the skin.

I yelped, jerking out of his arms; he seemed surprised, but after a moment he smiled at me, a shark's smile full of white teeth. He pulled my lip back into his mouth, gentle now, and sucked the blood from the cuts his incisors had made. Whatever. It wasn't the weirdest thing I'd done with a guy in bed.

When we were done he offered to cook me dinner.

"I wasn't sure you'd come over," he told me, his voice a low rumble as he fetched a pan from beneath the sink. "I thought maybe... maybe I'd frightened you." He fetched a piece of meat from the freezer and began to unwrap it from the thick white butcher's paper.

"I'm not so easily frightened." I watched from the bedroom as he dropped the flank into the skillet. A rich sizzling sound filled the luxury apartment. The smell of crisping meat made my mouth water.

"I thought as much." He tossed me a look over his shoulder, smiled devilishly, and cooked.

When it was done he brought one plate back to the bed. He stood there for a moment, staring down at me, his eyes unreadable.

"Ask me for it," he said flatly.

Men and their power. It was something I'd grown to expect. Doesn't matter what they tell you in those feminist blogs on Tumblr, sometimes you have to get on your knees to get what you want. And god damn did I want that promotion.

I slipped from beneath the sheets, crawling towards the edge of the bed like a cat, and smiled at him.

"Can I have some?" I parted my lips obediently.

He liked that, I could tell. Carefully, he speared a piece of meat and slid the fork into my waiting mouth.

The flavor was unlike anything I'd ever tasted before. It was both sweet and savory, just the right consistency, perfectly seasoned. An 8/10 in bed *and* he could cook? I had to be careful not to fall in love.

I ate each piece off the end of his fork until the plate was empty, and though I pride myself on staying trim, I was surprised to find I wanted more.

Instead, we fucked again.

I slipped out the next morning, silently, leaving my plate in the kitchen sink. I had my demands, that was for sure, but I could wait until the next time we met. This was a lead I wasn't so quick to bury.

It was, thank god, a Saturday, so I went home and slept for the rest of the morning. Something felt off, like I had the flu or I'd been out drinking, and I didn't wake up until almost two in the afternoon.

When I came to, my teeth ached.

It was a deep ache, one that permeated through my gums into the bed of my tongue. It felt like the first bite of too-sweet cotton candy, cloying and somehow sickly. I was nauseous.

I took careful sips of water. When it seemed safe I made a salad for an admittedly late lunch. Spring mix, a few pecans, drizzle of vinaigrette.

Moments later it all came right back up, a leafy mess of foam sick straight into the stainless steel of my kitchen sink.

We met again that night. He cooked more for me. I wolfed it down and it stayed in my stomach like a stone. I felt better, but only after I'd been with him.

I got the promotion, sure, but I started using an awful lot of sick days.

I couldn't drink water anymore. My mouth was constantly full of saliva. When I'd try to force water down my throat would close and cramp, painful spasms twisting my muscles into submission.

And food. My food kept coming up when it wasn't something he'd made. I grew dependent on him, begging for more of his cooking, asking for it like a good girl. I began to wonder if he'd poisoned me, but I couldn't figure out how he could affect the food in my own fridge. And if he *was* poisoning me, why was his food the only thing that made me feel human? It didn't make sense.

It all came together, though, in the end. It always does.

I came to see him one night, my body ravenous for his and my stomach growling like a mad dog, and I didn't bother to knock. I let myself in.

That was my mistake. Well, one of them.

I found him crouched over his elegant Italian marble kitchen island, teeth tearing away at meat — it didn't look like the meat he so carefully crisped for me on his stovetop, but something fleshy and streaked with red. Something raw.

I called his name and he looked up at me, scraps of meat hanging from his mouth, looking more like a wolf than ever.

A very long moment passed between us before he spoke.

"This is what you asked for," he growled, dark eyes peering at me from beneath the same salt-and-pepper brows, hands stained with blood.

"I don't understand," I told him. But I did.

"You've been feeling it," he said. "The ache. The want. I know you have."

"I don't think we should see each other anymore," I murmured, and I meant it, but god how my mouth was watering.

His dark eyes bored into my skull. He speared a piece of the raw meat with his fork and held it out towards me.

"You asked for this," he whispered.

I didn't want to eat it. It was raw meat. It was dangerous. And so why was saliva filling my mouth, why were my teeth aching, why was I already taking the steps towards him, closing the gap between me and his cold Italian marble island?

I took the fork. My hand shaking, I put the meat into my mouth.

It was *incredible.*

I'm no food critic so I can't describe it, not really; it was like nothing I'd ever eaten before, nothing I'd ever even imagined. It was like tasting the food of the gods.

He watched as I savored it. He drank in the sounds of my pleasure. I knew he was getting hard.

"It's so much better raw," he said softly, "isn't it?"

There was something in his voice that alarmed me. Or perhaps it was something in my brain, in my conscience. Maybe it was something even deeper than that.

I opened my eyes and looked at his plate. Looked at the hunk of meat he'd been ripping pieces from. There was a trail of blood from that piece to the sink nearby. My eyes followed it the way you watch a car wreck, knowing you're going to see something horrible and yet utterly unable to look away.

The blood ended in the sink, a thick red pool beneath another hunk of meat, this one more recognizable than the piece he was chewing from. An arm.

A woman's, from the look of the delicately-fingered hand. A cocktail ring glinted cheerily at me under his apartment's expensive lighting.

I wish I could tell you I gagged, I felt the rise of bile in my throat, but I didn't.

I wanted more.

Maybe it was that, the horrifying realization that I wanted to put that arm in my mouth and rip away at it with my teeth until there was nothing left but gleaming white bone, that got me going. I turned to leave and suddenly he was behind me, his strong hands gripping my arms, pulling me back against him. I felt the insistent pressure of his erection against the small of my back. My skin was slippery with blood where he grabbed me.

"You wanted this," he pleaded, trying to wrestle me back into the apartment. "You did, I know you did, I could sense your hunger from the moment I first saw you... you're like me, I know you are..."

I tore away from him with a cry, my heel kicking back into his crotch in one swift thrust, and then he was howling, a terrible keening sound as I fled for the elevator.

"*This is what you asked for!*" he screamed, over and over again.

I can still hear him.

I quit my job, I moved apartments. When I started spotting him across the street from my building, I left the city. I still worry he'll find me, that my ambition will one day seek me out and he'll feed me more of the meat he keeps in his freezer. Until then, I'm laying low, staying quiet.

But the ache... the way my teeth ache...

I know it's for the meat. It's all I can keep down but I don't want it. I'm so hungry but I don't want it.

And what's worse, I need...

I need to *bite*.

That's where this came from, I know it. From him. When he bit my lower lip. Something inside him got inside me, inside my blood stream. Some sickness. The closest thing I've come up with is rabies but that doesn't explain–

It doesn't explain *enough*.

And though it's there constantly, the gnawing pit of hunger in my stomach, that's not the worst of it. The need to bite, the need to *share*, share this this ache, this want... it's nearly unbearable.

That's why, last night, I pulled out all my teeth with a pair of pliers.

I didn't want this. I never wanted this.

Take a deep breath.

I think I've stopped it for now. I don't think it can spread. Except for him. If it resides in him like I think it does, this disease, the hunger for flesh and gore and bone...

Well, I'll put an end to that soon enough. Just as soon as my gums stop bleeding.

20

PREVIOUS OCCUPANTS

You never know who lived in your house before you moved in.

Isn't that strange? I mean, yeah, you might know the people who sold it to you, or the family who left just after you signed a new lease, but not the ones before them. Or the ones before them. Depending on how old your house is, people might have been walking around it in poodle skirts or zoot suits, lives that have already been started and ended before you were even born. Those people existed wherever you take a step in that house—they loved and lost and lived right where you set up your Playstation 4.

It may be strange, thinking of all the souls who lived there before, but it's better than knowing.

Believe me. It's better.

I should've been suspicious when I read the Zillow listing. "NOT a foreclosure, but PRICED like one!" Doesn't that just scream bad news? Not to me. I needed a place to live, you can't go on living without one, and this house was close enough to the university. "Updated nearly everything!" the listing said. Doesn't that make you wonder?

I don't have to.

The boy who used to live in my house, his name was Travis. His mom sent him to the Midwest from their place in Newark because he "needed straightening out."

His friends called him New Jersey. It was a tough-guy name, something that made him feel cool. He fell in with the wrong crowd because, well, Newark isn't the only place where kids can get into trouble.

There was a fight at school. He jumped in because, you know, it was his crew. He had a duty.

The fight was about a Walkman. Someone had stolen someone else's. Names were called, slurs were dropped, and then they had fought.

The rest of the guys, they got taken away to jail because they were of legal age, considered adults. Travis, though, he wasn't old enough. His 17th birthday was still on the horizon. The cops just sent him home early.

Word went around fast. New Jersey was a snitch. That's why he got to go home. He fought the rumors as best he could, but his former friend, the one who started the fight, this guy who thought himself something of a kingpin, well... he had it out for him.

Do you remember high school? Everything seems like the end of the world.

This guy, he told people he was gonna get Travis. He was gonna get him or he was gonna get someone else to do it for him.

Travis went to school. He came home from school. He did homework. He watched as all his friends sort of fell away.

One night, someone drove by the house. They shot through the living room window. The bullet went into the kitchen wall but you can't even see it now. Believe me, I've looked.

Travis's five-year-old brother had a birthday party. There were a ton of people there. You see, even though this place is just big enough for me, Travis had a lot of family. Too much for this little house. The adults were always going into the basement. I think it was for some pretty shady reasons. I don't go down there, the place is dark and damp and it feels like someone's watching you.

At the birthday party, someone knocked on the door. Travis's uncle answered it, and the kid there said hey, is Travis home? I want to talk to Travis.

Travis's uncle closed the door. He got Travis from his bedroom. The front door, the door to my house, it had these three little windows you could look right out and see who's on the porch. So they looked through the windows.

I don't know that guy, Travis told him. But he went outside anyway.

Travis's uncle kept looking through the window in the door. The kids talked. He waited a few minutes. Didn't look like anything bad, just two kids talking, so he turned back to the kitchen to get some cake.

Then Travis's uncle heard someone yell no! And pop, pop, pop. Real loud.

Before he could even turn back to the door Travis was falling through it, face-first onto the filthy brown carpet, a blossom of bright red blood blooming on his white t-shirt.

Little kids were screaming. His grandma was screaming. The guy on the porch was gone.

The fight was about a Walkman.

A stupid Walkman.

Like the listing said, nearly everything has been updated. You can't see the bullet holes. The brown carpet that turned a darker brown when Travis bled out, it was ripped up and replaced with an unassuming beige Berber. The front door, well, it doesn't have any windows.

These changes, these updates, they don't really change anything. They don't change what I know now about the place where I live, the place I'm supposed to feel safe. They don't change the fact that Travis died in the same spot I have to cross every day to get the mail.

I wish I would've known sooner, before I bought the place. Or that I didn't know at all. But I do. I do know.

Because every night, when I lay down to go to sleep, just when my eyes are shut and I think maybe that night could be different, Travis tells me the story all over again.

21

HAIMA

We should've used a condom. Don't tell me because I already know.

But you know, sometimes shit happens. You forget that your rubbers are expired or you send your prescription for birth control to the wrong Walgreens, the one way across town and it's just inconvenient to drive all that way, then your period comes and goes and you forget about it and then he's on top of you, you're pawing at each other on a lazy Sunday afternoon and...

Shit happens.

The next day all I could think was how we should've used a condom, how stupid it was, how the whole thing was preventable. My period was due to start any day now but I already had it in my mind that I'd fucked up my entire life; I was already pregnant. That's what they tell you in school, you know? Just one time, that's all it takes. It just seemed — what's the word? — inevitable.

You can't know you're pregnant a day after conception. Shit, your *body* doesn't even know yet. But already I was chewing my nails down to the quick, pacing my apartment, wondering how I was going to tell him, how we were going to make this work. I haven't been to church in over 15 years but I prayed for my period to come. Like, legit got down on my knees and prayed to the god of menstruation to please, please, save me from this one mistake so I could learn from it.

I stressed myself out so badly I got a nosebleed. So I tried to calm down, relax, not worry about it so much. I sat on the couch, held a tissue to my face, and watched "Mad Men".

The first day it wasn't so bad. Just a trickle, really. It would stop and start but it was over by the time I went to bed.

When I woke up the next morning my pillowcase was soaked in blood.

I could feel it on my upper lip, thick and tacky. It smelled like old pennies cradled in someone's sweaty palm. I got up fast, the blood still pouring from my nose, and hurried to the bathroom for more tissues. I went through a whole roll of toilet paper before the flow started to die down again.

Never had nosebleeds before. Not even in dry weather. I spent the rest of the week with tissues jammed up both nostrils, just trying to keep the bleeding at bay.

I should've told my boyfriend, I know that too, but I was embarrassed. He'd want to know why I was so stressed and I couldn't tell him, not yet, not when my period was only a few days late. I mean, I didn't *really* know yet, you know? I held the toilet paper to my nose and told myself that, that I didn't really know, while something deep inside my guts told me yes, I did.

At the end of week one, my trashcans were full of red-spotted tissue, but the cotton panel of my panties stayed pristine and white.

My nose stopped bleeding. Life went on.

I began to worry again, my period was over a week late now and I wasn't experiencing the typical PMS symptoms — no raging hormones, no insatiable hunger. But I got distracted again when one morning, after my shower, I cleaned my ears with q-tips that came back with blood on them.

This was harder to treat. Tissues wouldn't stay in there if I sat up but soon enough I found that cotton balls worked pretty well. It got hard to hear anyone who was talking to me, and the looks I got on the street were funny, so I just stayed home.

Endless crimson-soaked cotton balls in the trash, piling up like morbid little mountains.

Week two was over and my ears stopped bleeding. Still no period.

I began considering a procedure. I couldn't have a baby. Especially not in this condition.

Week three, I made an appointment at Planned Parenthood. I no more hit the 'end call' button on my phone before I felt a tickle in my throat.

Started coughing. Couldn't stop. I felt something rise in the back of my throat and just barely made it to the sink before I hacked up a chunk of thick, bloody discharge.

I stared at it for a long time. It looked like a lump of tissue, something vital and visceral. A few drops of blood peppered the white porcelain around it.

My nose started up again. And my ears. In the mirror, I was a monster from a horror movie.

I canceled my Planned Parenthood appointment and checked in online at urgent care. I called my boyfriend. I couldn't deny it any longer — something was really, really wrong.

Before he came to pick me up I did what I could — twisted tissues up each nostril, jammed the cotton balls in my ears. The coughing I couldn't really help, so I brought a coffee cup to spit in.

He was so upset. He kept looking at me as he drove like he couldn't believe what he was seeing.

The waiting room wasn't any better. People were staring at me — I felt like a freak show. I began to cry and wasn't even surprised when the tear that slipped down my cheek onto the back of my hand was a thick red drop.

The doctors seemed very concerned. Spoke in hushed whispers, first to each other, then my boyfriend. I guess they'd never had anyone with this particular problem before.

Finally, after what seemed like forever, one of them closed the door and sat down in front of me, his face serious as a stone.

He asked me to please take the cotton balls out of my ears and the tissues out of my nose. He asked me if I was ready to tell them when the hallucinations started.

I started to cry then, more blood streaming down my face and splashing onto my dress. How could they not see it? I tore the tissues from my nose and thrust them towards the doctor, took the cotton balls and hurled them across the room. Couldn't they see the gore, the blood that had tormented me from the start, gushing from every hole except the one that mattered?

I'm waiting for them to come back now. Alone in this stupid white room, sitting on the crinkly paper, wishing I hadn't thrown my tissues at the doctor because it's running out of my ears now, down my face, over my upper lip. I can taste it. Outside the door they're talking to my boyfriend, all I can catch is little snatches of unfamiliar words. "Ah-men-o-rea." "Soo-do-sy-sis."

"Hysterical." That one, I know.

They don't think I'm pregnant. But they don't think I'm bleeding, either.

So then why, even as I hear them talking in their hushed tones about involuntary committal and psych wards, even as the blood soaks my nice white dress, can I feel the movement in my stomach, the quick little fluttering of life deep inside me?

Don't tell me. I already know.

22

THE NIGHTMARE CLUB

———————

This isn't a story. This is a warning.

Forgive my brevity. There's not much time left. I read about an experiment once that said some kid in 1965 stayed awake for 11 days, set a world record, but I haven't slept in nearly a month and I'm afraid my breaking point is on the horizon.

You know those people who love to be scared? The ones who see every horror movie, read every Stephen King novel, jump out of airplanes just for the rush? Maybe you're one of them. I know I was.

It started simply enough. Another boring Saturday night surfing the internet and watching Netflix, because focusing your attention on one thing in this day and age is not only laughable, but impossible.

You never expect your life to change, you know? Especially not thanks to some stupid email.

Shit. I have to stay focused. It's hard to focus, though, it said so in that article about the kid in 1965, how there was no extensive damage to the people who stayed awake that long but their concentration broke down more and more as the days went on. It's almost like being a child again, the way your eyes and mind jump from subject to subject endlessly, endlessly.

Anyway. It was the email that started it all. I figured it was some new form of viral marketing, a program that was tracking my browser history and targeting me for a sale — hey, that stuff is out there, look it up if you don't believe me — and I nearly deleted it without reading.

I should have. I should have deleted it. I know that now.

But the subject was just too tantalizing. In all-caps, like some sort of electronic shout, it read:

SEARCHERS AFTER HORROR HAUNT STRANGE, FAR PLACES

What did it mean? Nothing really, I suppose, but the lyrical quality of the words and the vague promise they held urged me to click. So I did.

It was poorly constructed, just plaintext and odd, nonsensical line breaks:

> *if the only*
> > *thing to fear*
> > *is fear*
> *itself*
> *then why are you*
> > > *still*
>
> *here?*
> *4100 w pfeiffer rd*
> COME
> > *ALONE*

A quick plug of the address into Google brought up a place about 20 minutes from where I lived, an abandoned insane asylum. The building had been closed to the public for years, supposedly due to asbestos, but there were rumors that it was too haunted to restore as the buyers had previously hoped.

It was stupid. A prank. At the very least, some sort of trap, where I'd end up mugged and unconscious, a fitting punishment for someone who paid attention to emails like this.

I closed it. Watched more of the movie. Opened it again.

Something was tugging at me. Maybe the way it was constructed, the breaks without rhyme or reason, the musical sound of the subject line. Searchers after horror.

Strange, far places.

It was after midnight but I grabbed my keys, put the address into my iPhone, and heeded the email's advice — I went alone.

The turn-by-turn directions landed me in the middle of an industrial park, right in front of the hulking monstrosity of a building. It was in a state of disrepair, the windows closest to the ground boarded up to discourage trespassers. The rest of the windows were like dead, staring eyes, half-open and full of shattered glass.

Okay. Off to a good start. Definitely scary. But I'll admit, at the moment my biggest fear was being caught by the cops.

I sat in my car for a little while, unwilling to approach the building without proof that someone was waiting for me, until the thick rusted bars of the front door swung open and a hand beckoned.

Ooo. Spooky.

Just like an idiot in a horror movie I got out of the car and hightailed it up the front steps. I don't know what I expected, maybe someone dressed like the Grim Reaper or wearing a Scream mask, but waiting inside was just a regular-looking guy with an Arcade Fire t-shirt.

"You made it," he said, grinning.

"How do you know I'm the right person?" I pocketed my car keys as he shut the door behind me with a clang.

"You were tonight's target," the guy explained, and when I frowned he laughed a little. "Our target demo. You've been on our radar for a while. Internet cookies, you know? I've seen your Facebook, I recognized you."

See? What did I tell you? *That* shit is what's really scary.

The inside of the place was ransacked; the paint peeled off the walls in thick curling chips, flaking down to the floor where feeble grass grew through the cracks. Above one of the doorways that led further inside some genius had spraypainted "HELL AWAITS." A nice touch.

"We're glad you showed up," the guy said suddenly, drawing my attention away from the doorway. "We've only got a 2% conversion rate, which is great in most businesses but not very efficient in what we do."

He kept saying "we," but I didn't see anyone else around.

"What exactly *do* you do?" When I glanced back at his face I realized how tired he looked, like he'd just pulled an all-nighter or something. The guy laughed again.

"We specialize in what you want," he said breezily. "Fear."

For a moment he didn't say anything else. His eyes had gone somewhat distant, like someone had unplugged him and all the machinery was shutting down. I was suddenly sure that I was going to be murdered and left in a ditch somewhere, but the guy snapped out of it and turned to a black backpack resting against the wall.

"Take these." He fished around for a moment and produced a small pill-holder, the generic plastic kind you can buy at Walgreens with all of the days portioned out neatly for the whole week. In each section there was a small round pill. It reminded me of the percocet I took when I had my wisdom teeth removed.

"I'm not gonna just take some pills from a stranger, man," I told him, but he had already put the container into my hand.

"Yeah," he said simply. "You are."

The guy turned away and shouldered his backpack. I saw that he meant to leave, looked at the pills again, and followed him to the door.

"Hey! Wait!" I grabbed him by the shoulder and turned him to face me. "I don't know what all this is, but I'm *not* taking these pills—"

"You have to." The guy looked mildly alarmed, his eyes darting all over my face. The bags under them were like bruises. "You're the target, it's what you like, we know it is. You *like* to be scared. So you'll take the pills, but only one a day. Or night. Whatever." He shrugged away from me and headed for the door again.

When he reached it, he paused. His head turned back to me.

"Best to take one right away," he murmured thoughtfully. "No sense in waiting." Then, just like that, he was gone.

I stood there, alone, for quite some time. I stared at the pill container in my hand.

This whole thing was stupid, I remember thinking how stupid it was even as I opened that day's section and dumped the pill into my palm. Even as I opened my mouth and dry-swallowed the little white tablet, I was thinking, this is so stupid.

It was only after the pill was down my throat and gone that I realized what I'd done. I felt vaguely like one of the characters in Lovecraft's stories, the ones where a hapless young man is drawn into a situation that's clearly dangerous, like going to a remote cabin in the woods or having sex with a witch.

I thought about forcing myself to throw it up, but before I knew it I was back in my car, driving the 20 minutes towards home. When I got there it was nearly two in the morning; I kicked off my shoes and collapsed into bed.

That night, I had the most horrific nightmares.

I never had nightmares, rarely dreamt at all — usually, the worst of them involved being back in college and taking a test I hadn't studied for — but that night was different. I can't remember them all, but in one I was being slowly eaten alive by a grey skeletal creature, a sharp-toothed grimacing smile on its face as I screamed and screamed and it licked my blood from its fingers.

In another, I lived in a high-rise building that hadn't been constructed properly; every time I tried to cross the room the entire structure shook, threatening to collapse all of its hundreds of stories with me inside.

When I finally woke the next morning I was absolutely drenched in sweat. My heart raced wildly in my chest. The terror from those awful dreams still crawled through my skin even though I was awake, I knew I was awake, I touched my face and the sheets as proof.

Best to take one right away. The guy's voice echoed in my head. Was that what did it? The pill? He'd been so insistent, so *sure* I'd take it. And damn it, I did.

What was their angle? They found people online, gave them free pills that caused nightmares? What the fuck kind of sense did that make?

Well, one thing was for certain — I wasn't going to take another one.

That night, I swallowed the second pill and chased it with vodka.

I wish I could explain why I took it. I wish I could explain it to you but I'm so goddamn tired.

The second night was worse. The nightmare was like a film that kept skipping; I was being pursued by something through a dark tangle of woods, I kept tripping and falling but it never quite caught up to me. When I hit the ground something would chuckle softly nearby, too nearby, so I would scramble to my feet and keep going. Just when the woods seemed to clear the dream would shudder and suddenly I was back at the beginning.

When I woke up it was like I hadn't slept at all. I was mentally exhausted, so godawful tired that I called in sick to work that day.

And the day after that. Because that night, I took another pill.

It went on that way until the pills were gone. I was like a heroin junkie chasing a fix; I couldn't stop. As long as there were pills in the container, I took them. It was an indescribable relief to realize one day that they were all gone, that they didn't have power over me anymore.

I called my job and promised I'd be in the next day. I took a long, hot shower. I watched a nice romantic comedy on Netflix, something where no one was being tortured or murdered. I drank a mug of peppermint tea.

That night was the worst yet. Even without the pills, the nightmares not only continued, they intensified. Now when I hit the ground I could feel the brittle branches beneath my hands, when the grey creature ate away at my feet it actually hurt.

The morning I woke up missing the big toe from my left foot, well, that was when I knew I was in trouble.

I couldn't go to the doctor — there was no explanation for why there was a bloody stump where my toe had once been. Besides, what if he asked about the pills? How was I supposed to tell him that I'd been taking pills for a week when I didn't even know what they were? And really, it wasn't like they could reattach my toe. It wasn't broken, it was just *gone*, most likely in the belly of the grinning grey monster that waited for me in my nightmares.

Maybe that makes sense. Maybe it doesn't. Things stop making much sense after a few days without sleep.

Because that was the only answer, you know? Don't sleep. If you don't sleep, you can't have nightmares. It all seemed so simple.

I drank coffee. I bought a case of those Five Hour Energy things. Red Bull and cold showers. I kept a tack in my shoe so when I felt myself drifting off I could step down on it. The pain always brought me back.

Like I said, it's been almost a month. I feel like I'm losing it. Can't even look in a mirror for fear of what I might see staring back at me.

I've thought about it a lot. There's no way to trace the guy, or the email they sent me, but I've thought about it.

The guy, he was tired too. So tired. But not as tired as me. Because I think he figured it out. He went back to whoever gave him the pills, asked how to make it stop.

They had to find someone like me. Someone who foolishly loved fear, someone to whom the call of the dark would be irresistible.

And, as all tyrants and dictators already know, fear spreads.

The one thing I can't figure out is *why*.

I need to finish this up because I really don't think I can do it anymore. I need to sleep, no one can stay awake forever, but I'm so scared. I'm scared because this time I think I'll lose more than just a toe.

So like I said. This isn't a story. It's a warning. Because if you're here, reading this now, you're on their radar.

You're here because you like fear.

But you have no idea. You have no idea what true fear is.

Don't open the email. Don't meet them anywhere. Don't take the pills.

Strange, far places.

I have to go now.

Be safe.

About the Author

Photography by Lisa Lilburn

M.J. Pack is Creepy Catalog's horror writer who is currently haunting St. Louis. She loves found footage scary movies, the collective works of Stephen King, and things that go bump in the night.

50288738R00134

Made in the USA
Charleston, SC
20 December 2015